FIDDLE MAGIC

The street fiddler was squatting by the open violin case, fishing out the money. I got the nerve to walk right up and talk to him.

"Hi," I said. "Thanks for helping yesterday in the subway."

"Good thing you got in touch," he said. "We knew there was something wrong, but we didn't know where."

"I didn't know I got in touch. How did I do that?"

"The way your granny taught you," he said.

Make a wish by running water and seal it with silver.

"Oh!" I said. See, when I was little, Granny Gran used to do sort of magic things. Whenever I asked her how she did those things, she'd say, "Oh, it's something I learned in Sorcery Hall."

That's why I said, "You must be from Sorcery Hall! Are you looking for Granny Gran?"

He shook his head. "I'm looking for you. I need your help."

"Help with what?"

"Well," he said, "you got a kraken here."

"What's a kraken?"

He rubbed the side of his neck. "Okay. It's a negative interstitial vortex with a big appetite. It's going to try to eat up your world if we don't stop it. . . ."

Other Bantam Starfire Books you will enjoy

HAVE A HEART, CUPID DELANEY by Ellen Leroe
FINGERS by William Sleator
ANYTHING FOR A FRIEND by Ellen Conford
HAIL, HAIL CAMP TIMBERWOOD by Ellen Conford
PERSONAL BUSINESS by Ellen Leroe
SHADOW OF A UNICORN by Norma Johnston
WATCHER IN THE MIST by Norma Johnston
HAUNTED by Judith St. George
ON THAT DARK NIGHT by Carol Beach York

THE BRONZE KING

Suzy McKee Charnas

BANTAM BOOKS
TORONTO • NEW YORK • LONDON • SYDNEY • AUCKLAND

RL 5, IL age 11 and up

THE BRONZE KING

A Bantam Book / published by arrangement with Houghton Mifflin Company

PRINTING HISTORY

Houghton Mifflin edition published October 1985
Bantam Skylark edition / April 1987
Bantam Starfire edition / March 1988

ISBN 0-553-27104-0

Published simultaneously in the United States and Canada

PRINTED IN THE UNITED STATES OF AMERICA

O   0 9 8 7 6 5 4 3 2 1

Acknowledgments

Grateful acknowledgment is hereby made to various people in the New York subway system who provided information used in this story, and to Greg Sandow who knew something about that system that outsiders are not supposed to know; to Quinn Yarbro for help with magic and lots else; to Vonda McIntyre and other early readers and hearers of this tale for their comments and responses; and to the two Lindas and everybody else in Word Processing for their patient help. In addition, I owe an acknowledgment to whoever first used the eighteenth-century Norwegian word kraken *to name an interstellar monster-type heavy. John Wyndham's* Out of the Deeps *(published in England as* The Kraken Wakes*), circa 1953, has been suggested as the source. In any case, it's a lovely usage, gratefully borrowed.*

This book is dedicated with the warmest appreciation to classical musicians. These performers must know better than anyone what is magical in music, what is plain hard work, and what somehow manages to be both. I am particularly indebted to the people I've had the pleasure of listening to live, in concert and in rehearsal, these many summers at the Santa Fe Chamber Music Festival. For their efforts, which are always interesting and sometimes a form of healing and nourishing wizardry, much gratitude, of which this dedication stands as a token.

Contents

THE BRONZE
KING

1
Tuna Fish

Things started to disappear the day of the explosion in the subway station. (At least, that was Tuesday morning and at lunch period I discovered that my tuna fish sandwich was missing.)

First though, there was this explosion. I was heading for school, trying to ignore the miserable time I knew was coming up in math class. A test was scheduled soon and I was worried. I stopped to lean on the metal skirting around the entrance to the Eighty-first Street subway station on Central Park West, and I dug around in my bookbag for the piece of paper where I'd written down some questions about the review assignment.

All of a sudden the sidewalk jumped under my feet and there was this deep, low, far-off *whoof,* like one giant bark from a monster hound in the center of the earth.

Earthquake, I thought, the end! I'll never have to take a math test again. Something hard and small dinged me on the forehead, just over my left eye, and I blinked, and that was it. No smoke, no yelling, nobody running, just me standing there on the sidewalk next to the subway entrance across from the park and rocking a little.

Still alive, I thought, rats! There is no escape. I took the bus across the park to school. Nobody else at school knew anything about an explosion in the subway. I started thinking I'd dreamed it. Maybe I'd had a moment of mental fugue, which seems to mean nuttiness, imagining what I would like to do to math as a subject: blow it up.

At lunch, it was my sandwich that was gone. I had to spend allowance money on school cafeteria slop, which I did not like because I am picky about what I put in my stomach except for special days when I declare a junk-food blitz. I tried to make this into one of those days, but not very successfully. The stuff in the school cafeteria isn't nice, spicy, fattening junk. It's just crud.

My best friend Megan sat with me at lunch, but she might as well have been on the moon. She was madly in love with a boy named Micky in the grade ahead of us and wouldn't talk about anything else. In fact she had begun treating me like a baby for not being all dopey over some boy myself, and we had not been hanging around together much lately.

My other best friend, Barbara, had suddenly started getting into her roots, which meant wearing her hair in cornrows and talking street Black and hanging around with a very slick clique that didn't welcome white kids. So I was pretty much on my own with this disappearing problem. It made me so nervous that I took the bus home too, instead of walking through the park as I usually did if the weather was nice.

That evening, I told Mom about the explosion and she fussed and patted me all over to make sure I was all right. Since I was, she forgot all about it. She was in a burn about the landlord and how our building was going to hell. That's what was mostly on her mind these days, which suited me. It kept her from riding me.

All through dinner I heard about how the evening doorman was being replaced again as part of the land-lord's systematic effort to force us all to move out so he could turn the place into a luxury condo. I tried to get interested. I was, in a way. I sure did not want to go and live in the Bronx like Mom was always threatening we would have to.

Anyway, with one thing and another, I forgot about the subway explosion.

I did notice though, before I went to bed, that the knob was missing from the closet door in my bedroom.

"Well, look around for it," Mom said, when I told her. "Find it and call up Sam to come put it back on."

Sam was our building's handyman, and he was pretty hard to find himself a lot of the time. The doorknob was impossible. I gave up.

The next morning my sneakers were gone. I mean gone, disappeared. Not my new sneaks, but my old beat-up ones that I wore all summer in camp. I was really upset. It was not great, having to go to school in my stiff new running shoes instead of my sneaks. I'd been saving the new ones for some special occasion.

Everything that had gone on so far had to do with me. Was it my fault somehow? Was I supposed to be putting out a dish of milk for the leprechaun? When I was little I kept a little bed and tiny cardboard furniture in the drawer of the old drop leaf table in the hall for the elf I made believe lived there. That was years ago. But now I kept thinking, Is it something I did? That's exactly the kind of question Dr. Morely got me to quit asking about things that plainly were other people's business—like my parents' divorce—when I spent a large part of my third-grade year talking with her.

So it's not surprising I actually thought about calling up Dr. Morely about the disappearances. She's pretty good, though of course you can never tell if you got better on your own or because of a shrink. But I didn't want my mom involved, and Dr. Morely cost more than my allowance would buy.

Anyway, the disappearing problem was on my mind all the way through school that day, and on into the park on my way home afterwards.

I always walk between the Metropolitan Museum on one side and the playground on the other, and down under the stone arch and up again to cross the center of the park. That's the high part that has the statue of King Jagiello at its eastern edge and the little Belvedere Castle and the Delacorte Theatre on the western edge, with the shallow lake between them. The big open playing field runs north from the lake, and sometimes people play soccer there, which I love to look at. It's a graceful game, not like mad-bull football which I mainly like to watch when I am furious about something.

Then I go down the hill past the stone cottage with the rest rooms in it, across the bridle path, and out past the other playground to the West Side. From there, it's only a few blocks to home.

Today I came out from under the stone arch and there was a crowd milling around on the rise to my left, on Jagiello's paved terrace. Two police cars and a Parks Department truck were parked on the stone flagging at that end of the lake, where all of a sudden I noticed that there was no statue of Jagiello.

Now, I am not talking about some little figurine here that a person could stick in their pocket and take home. I'm not even talking about something like the duck that somebody sawed off the Hans Christian Andersen statue down by the boat pond and stole (but it was found and put back later). The statue of Jagiello is a bigger-than-life-size horse carrying a huge bronze warrior in armor and a great big flowing bronze cape. This medieval king on horseback holds up two swords with their blades crossed high over the head of his horse, sort of like somebody fending off a vampire with the sign of the cross.

This was my favorite statue in the park, maybe because it was ugly and lumpy and there was something wrong with the perspective of the horse's back legs. But in spite of that people always stopped and looked. They walked around and read the inscription on the pink marble block the horse stood on and they took pictures. Everybody stopped and took notice of Jagiello.

Only today they were taking notice of where Jagiello used to be but wasn't anymore. The pink marble block was bare on top.

I couldn't believe it. We all have to put up with a lot of vandalism in the park, but this was too much.

"What's everybody staring at?" somebody next to me said.

It was Megan. She still walked home with me sometimes, the way we used to, if Micky was busy or had stood her up or whatever. Today she was red in the face and miserable-looking, which meant that Micky was doing one of his numbers on her. Why she put up with him I could not imagine, but at least I wouldn't have to hear all about it, because here was something different and much more interesting to talk about.

"Jagiello's gone," I said.

"That ugly old statue? So what? They probably took it down to clean it."

"Then what are all these cops doing here?" I said.

What they were doing was measuring things and taking pictures and talking on their two-way radios.

"Move along, please," a cop with a megaphone said. "It's all over; we think the statue's been missing at least a day, so there's nothing to see and you're blocking the pedestrians."

"We *are* pedestrians," I said, but not loud. I'd seen the statue on Monday. So it was gone since sometime yesterday, I thought, like everything else that was missing. That it hadn't been officially noticed until today was just— well, New York.

Megan said, "Probably somebody forgot to pass along some stupid piece of paper telling everybody where the statue was being taken, that's all."

"No," I said, as we walked on. "Things are disappearing."

"Sure," she said. "Like you, when you're supposed to be waiting for me in the library. It's Wednesday, remember? What about the test tomorrow?"

I had completely forgotten the test. Megan had agreed to go over some math notes with me. But there was no way I could do that now, not once I'd started on the subject of the disappearances.

I told her about what was gone, including first thing this morning the medicine cabinet from the big bathroom. Mom was sure the landlord had sent Sam the handyman sneaking in at night to do this, like some demented burglar, to make us move out.

Now, this is not as crazy as it sounds if you keep up with the landlord-tenant wars in New York, as Megan pointed out. She reads the *Village Voice* religiously, and that paper is really hipped on this particular subject.

I wasn't worried about that, though I couldn't say exactly what it was I was worried about. I told her how Mom had tried to get hold of Sam to get the lowdown from him—he was friendly. Only Sam hadn't been around this morning either.

Megan said, "Oh, come on, a pair of sneakers, a handyman hiding from a pissed-off tenant. An apartment hassle, that's all you've got."

"And Jagiello."

"Look, I turned down a chance to go down to the arcades with Micky to come looking for you. You want to do some math today or not?"

Which meant Micky had left her behind, in his usual casual fashion, and I was about to get told all about it in an edited version as clear as glass. Which I could not stand, because Megan always ended up figuring out that I knew what was really going on and telling me anyway and crying. I just wasn't up to all that, and it made me mad to have her always set it up as if she were doing me a favor. All she was really doing was pinning me down so she could cry and swear about Micky to somebody.

"No," I said. "I'm going on home, Megan. I've got a lot to think about." And I wanted to see if anything else had disappeared while I'd been in school.

"Yourself, you mean," Megan said, stopping dead in that stubborn way she had. "As usual. That's all you ever think about anymore. Well, go ahead, but don't expect me to walk with you. I've got lots of better things to do. And don't come moaning to me when you fail that test, either!" She turned and headed back toward school, where I guessed she would try to find out where Micky had gone and go trailing after him.

I went past the theater and started down the west side of the big hill, and a guy on a skateboard came grinding past and tried to grab my pocketbook.

I yelled, yanked back on the strap, and fell into some bushes. The guy put on more speed and went roaring down the hill, across the roadway, and right down to the bridle path, where he jumped off, stuck the board under his arm, and ran away out of the park.

I stood there, rubbing my knee and yelling after him. Of course the cops didn't come—they were all busy looking for Jagiello and what's a kid yelling, anyhow?

I'd torn my jeans and scraped my knee in falling. One more patch to sew on.

I headed home, but slowly. I didn't want to run into that guy again. It was funny how shaky I felt, considering all I had was a fall. It hadn't even been as bad as getting knocked down in a basketball game.

But I could still see that guy on his board, a skinny kid wearing a gray nylon jacket with a black skull and lettering on the back that read PRINCE OF DARKNESS, speeding away from me on his wheels, sort of graceful like somebody riding a surfboard, and not looking back.

2
Creeps

Next morning, Mom left me a note: "We're out of paper towels, detergent, sugar, and coffee. Please use note as basis for shopping list. Also no jelly. Bread without jelly = morning without sunshine. Please fix. Mom. P.S. You're on your own tonight, editorial conference."

Which meant *a,* that she would be having dinner with one of the senior editors. which meant pretty soon she'd start bringing him home and I'd have to "relate" to him somehow or other; and *b,* that when she'd left for work, the linoleum was still on the kitchen floor, or she would have mentioned it. All I found there was this disgusting dried-up black glue to walk on. I mean she would have hit the ceiling so you could hear it on the East Side.

So it's not surprising that I flunked the math test. All I could think about was the kitchen floor: that and what else might suddenly disappear. Suppose somebody decided to "take" the whole sixth floor of my building, and suppose I was home at the time?

Not that there was any sensible reason to take our apartment, but what was sensible about taking the linoleum from our kitchen floor?

School was a dull blur that day, except for that nightmare math test. I dawdled home through the park, thinking about the careers open to people who simply never got out of school as a result of being math imbeciles; and also about the fireworks there would be when Mom finally did find the kitchen floor in its current state. I thought about calling her up to warn her. If she turned up with Mr. Whoever and he saw the state of that floor, she'd be fit to be tied, and I couldn't blame her. I mean, I didn't much like her taste in men, but I hated to see her embarrassed.

I couldn't help wondering if the whole thing had something to do with Jagiello, but what? Without him, the whole park felt different to me

It felt emptier, colder, with bigger spaces between one person and the next. Everybody I could see looked really alone out there.

There's a wide open space up by the lake. You can see people a long way off. This time I kept my eyes open and I looked around behind me now and then just to make sure nobody was sneaking up on me.

Nobody was. Nobody was anywhere near me. I might have been in Death Valley.

I started to have this headache and this wobbly feeling inside like I was about to cry. Maybe I would end up crippled with migraines, the way my Granny Gran was sometimes. A thing like that could be hereditary, couldn't it? That thought really scared me.

Granny Gran was off in a rest home in New Jersey. Her name is really Grandmother Grahame, but she was Granny Gran the way I was Tina to my relatives and friends, rather than Valentine. She was no longer compos mentis all the time, and Mom couldn't stay home and take care of her or afford a nurse to do it. I loved Granny Gran a lot, but I didn't get to see her much anymore.

I walked to the edge of the lake in front of Jagiello's terrace, where some low black rocks stick out into the water. The lake was muddy brown and not very deep, so I could see the trash sunk in it—old paper cups and cigarette packs and some kind of twisted wire and so on. People are such slobs.

Boy, did my head hurt.

Make a wish, said something inside my head. Granny Gran used to say that: make a wish by running water and seal it with silver.

Well, the lake water ran from somewhere. You could stand above the pipes that fed it from the middle of the north shoreline.

"Jagiello," I said, "come back and get things fixed the way they belong."

I flipped a dime into the filthy water and waited for something to happen.

What happened was that a crazy guy came stumping past me, talking a mile a minute to himself and anybody else close enough to hear. He announced in a loud voice, "You know who comes here? Thieves and degenerates and prostitutes come here, that's who comes here, and you know why? Because this is where Eve sinned. I don't know the exact spot, but it was right around here someplace."

That was all I needed. I headed home.

After I got some groceries at the store, I lay down in my room and read a book. I had an armload of books from the public library, mostly what they call "high fantasy," like Tolkien's books—full of prophecies, dethroned kings, magical swords, treasures, and battles with huge evil forces. No wonder Megan laughed at me and my "disappearances." And yes, the kitchen floor was just as I had found it that morning. Fortunately, my mom got home so late that night that she didn't notice at all.

I always know when she comes home. New York is a dangerous place, and just because the men she goes out with are usually connected in some way with the magazine she works for doesn't mean that they have to be particularly okay or responsible.

So I sort of sleep very lightly and don't really drop off until I hear her come in. It's a habit from when I was still little enough to need a baby sitter and I really thought sometimes Mom wouldn't ever come home.

At least this guy tonight brought her to the door, and in fact inside, and then things got very quiet, which I didn't like—it gave me the creeps, so I yanked the pillow around my head with both my elbows as clamps to keep out any sound, and I slept.

My mom and dad had had a very uncivilized divorce with lots of yelling and crying and doorslamming and everybody hugging the life out of me all the time and assuring me that it wasn't my fault, though I was pretty small and mostly didn't know what they were talking about.

Then he moved to Alaska and married a lady out there who had three kids of her own. The one time I visited was a disaster, so I didn't mind that I never went again. Their phone was always getting disconnected and they moved a lot, and he stopped writing after the third letter, so that was sort of that.

Mom and I hardly ever talked about him anymore, and to tell the truth I didn't think about him much. Mom still did, though, sometimes, judging from things she said. And she worried about me and boys.

I wonder what she would have said if she knew how I worried about her and men? I mean, staying up till she came home? It's not the kind of thing you can exactly talk about with your mom, so I never did.

If anything new was missing that Saturday morning, I didn't notice. I was tired and cranky and I spent most of the day hanging around in the corner store and browsing the magazines and the paperbacks, flipping through for the good parts. They knew me down there and they let me browse in exchange for my buying a chocolate malted, which they make very well. My metabolism handles any number of malteds without blinking. There are girls in school who would kill for my metabolism.

Sunday morning there wasn't a single Sunday *Times* outside the door of any apartment on our floor. I opened the door to get ours, and there was the Sneezer, our across-the-hall neighbor, with his head stuck out. He gave me this suspicious squint, as if I'd taken my paper and his, too.

We call him the Sneezer because he has allergies in the spring, and you can hear his thunderous sneezes three floors down in the elevator.

Then Mrs. Singh opened her door and glanced reproachfully out over her empty doormat at both of us, and I made a strategic withdrawal. Later I ran down to the corner store and got a *Times* for us, and Mom never knew anything about it. I made waffles for breakfast and read and brooded a lot.

The thing that struck me was that the magic in the stories I read was so—well, so *colorful.* Missing linoleum is not colorful. Only my mother's language on the subject was. I felt baffled and scared about whatever it was that was going on here. I couldn't think about it a whole lot at a time without getting really nervous.

Monday did not begin very well. I came in for some teasing by Kim Larkin and her pals, which sometimes happened probably because I was on my own a lot. I had had a couple of really good friends in the early grades in my school, but two had moved away and one had transferred to a parochial school and didn't keep in touch. Lately I'd sort of wandered out in left field someplace, what with Megan mooning over Micky all the time and Barbara avoiding me. Kim was the school clique-queen, if you know what I mean, and since Megan and Barbara had begun drifting off, Kim had started picking on me or sending her drones to do it for her. I guess that's how Kim's crowd reminded each other what hotshots they were.

They liked to tease me about my name, Valentine Marsh, saying things like, "Hey, Tina, how does Lennie like kissing mud?" Real heavy intellectual stuff.

Lennie was this very nice, big, lunky, shy boy I'd had a couple of dates with. We started out pretty badly. I got things mixed up and waited in the wrong place for him for a half hour, so instead of going to a movie with him I called up my mom crying to come and get me, which was pretty awful. Then Lennie and I went to a party and while we were dancing my glasses fell off and he stepped on them. We made a sort of mutual decision to call it a day, I guess, though I should have been grateful: it turned out I didn't need glasses anymore.

So anyway, Kim's crowd would make these stupid remarks which luckily ignored our real embarrassments, which nobody knew about because I would rather have died than tell (and I suppose the same was true of Lennie). I could never come up with anything smart to snap back, not until afterwards, naturally. Only once I said, "Go boil your head, maybe the freckles will come off," to Amy, Kim's right-hand jerk, but it didn't get me anywhere.

I think mainly I was just paralyzed by the injustice of it. As if Lennie and I were carrying on a wild affair or something! Which sometimes worried me, too, because when was this stuff with boys going to start making sense to me—without turning me into a burbling idiot like Megan? I mean, I knew I'd have to get into all this stuff sometime in a real way, but I did not want to leave my brain behind the way Megan had, and the way sometimes it almost seemed my mom herself still did. Some of the men Mom brought around! It was all still very much a mess and a puzzle and fearsome to me, and I guess you could say this was not a particularly smooth time in my life.

Kim and her buddies didn't make it any better, is what I'm trying to say.

At any rate, I needed some decent company that day so I went home with Margie Acton, a girl who was okay but not somebody to spend a lot of time with. She was very timid and neurotic and she pushed too hard to have you like her, maybe because she was from the Midwest and people called her a hick and said dumb, outrageous things all the time to try to shock her. Her parents were a pair of pills which I guess she couldn't do much about, but it did make it hard to hang around at her place.

I couldn't tell her anything about what was going on. She'd have leaked it to her mother, and her mother would have called up my mother. Mrs. Acton was one of those mothers who thought it was her job to get involved in everybody's life. It just wasn't worth the hassle to talk to Margie about the disappearances. We put on her records and played Battleship all afternoon, and then I went home.

Margie lived in Peter Cooper Village. I had to take the subway home.

Something happened.

It was just the kind of thing that Margie and her parents are terrified of about New York, but real New Yorkers get used to it early and hardly pay any attention. We know we can handle it.

Ha.

Three punky guys, about sixteen or seventeen I think, got on my subway car, looking for trouble. You could tell by the way they talked so loud and eyed everybody in that screw-you way that's meant to scare you.

The door near me, to the next car, was jammed. Some people in the car used the door at the other end to leave, but for me to get there, I would have to pass right by these creeps.

One of them turned around. He was wearing a gray nylon jacket with a black skull on it and the words PRINCE OF DARKNESS. They were all wearing gray nylon jackets.

The creeps started swinging on the holding bars like monkeys and kicking the seats. A man near them quit hiding behind his paper and got off at the next stop.

I should have too, but I only had one stop to go and I was late already and why should I get chased off my train and have to wait for another one just because some creeps got on? It was just a lousy coincidence. I thought that the one who had tried to grab my purse was the skinny one with the tattoo—a snake-mouth open wide with fangs sticking out—on his cheek. There was something about the way he stood, as if he was balanced on a surfboard. Probably, I told myself, he grabbed purses all the time; he wouldn't even remember me. I hugged my bag in my lap and sat tight. Mistake.

Between stations the train idled along and then stopped dead in the dark tunnel.

Nobody was in the car now but me and a sleeping drunk and these guys in their jackets and their chains looping down from their belts and their studded wrist straps and all the crap that guys like that like to wear. One of them had little enameled badges pinned all over the leather hat he was wearing, and he saw me looking and gave me a sideways grin. The third one chewed his gum and looked sleepy.

They started hassling the drunk, yelling in his ear and laughing and propping him up and sliding him down again on the seat. Pins-and-Grins went through the poor guy's pockets, making fun of finding nothing but holes and some pipe cleaners in there. The drunk was out of it, completely helpless, and the creeps were rough.

"Hey," Pins-and-Grins said, looking straight at me, "we got a class act in here with us, not like this old bum. Look at the little princess visiting the common people. Long as she's on our turf, we should show her a good time, right?"

I was really scared now. Was it better to yell some put-down at them, if I could think of one, to make them think I wasn't afraid? Or just pretend I didn't hear what they said? If only the train would start at least! Having a transit patrolman or a conductor show up was too much to hope for.

The Chewer shifted his gum to his other cheek. "That's her," he said.

"Sure it's her," Tattoo said. "And she's got something for us, right?"

I was whizzing over in my head what there was in my pocketbook that they could take—a couple of dollars, my tortoiseshell comb from Uncle Tim, my key ring with the souvenir medal from Colossal Cave that I'd found in a gas station rest room in the country—

They ambled down the car and stood over me. "Give it here," Tattoo said.

I clutched my bag and glared at him with my eyes all hot. The last thing I wanted to do was cry in front of these creeps, but I was scared. The Chewer grabbed my wrist hard enough to hurt.

"I don't have anything you want," I said.

"She don't have anything," the Chewer said in this disgusted voice. "Man, a princess shouldn't tell lies. It'll grow hair on the palms of her hands. Let's see if it's happening already."

He started to turn my hand over, and I knew he'd do something horrible, and Pins-and-Grins was reaching for my purse. And all of a sudden the jammed door next to me opened and a man stepped through, playing a violin.

It was the craziest thing—I mean, in the subway where you can hardly hear yourself think, here was this stranger fiddling like mad, some kind of jumping, gypsy sort of tune, full of throaty swoops and high, sweet curlicues that filled the whole car.

"What the hell?" yelped Tattoo, looking as if a flashbulb had gone off in his face.

"Well, come on," the Chewer said impatiently, and he pulled me up off the seat and started to dance with me.

I mean really dance—a hopping, jumping, racing-along, three-beat gallop, with our elbows stuck out and lots of space between us. The weirdest part was not that the train suddenly started going, as if our dancing had moved it, but that I knew the steps. Or anyway I did the steps, though in my head I didn't know how to dance any better than I ever did.

We went cavorting up and down the subway car like a couple of loonies, him reeking of some supermacho musk and beer and staring off over my shoulder as if I wasn't there, and me with my purse banging me on the hip.

The other two stood and clapped their hands in time to the music, which sounded loud and clear over the rattle of the train.

I was completely zonked myself and bubbling inside with joy because I knew I was safe. The music promised me that. I heard Tattoo yell to his buddy, "What a crazy old fart, playing the fiddle in the subway!" But he kept on clapping, and we kept dancing, until the train pulled into my station. Then the fiddler quit playing and whipped the cap off his headful of curly gray hair and held it out for them to put money in.

The doors opened. The Chewer, panting hard from all that jumping around, let go of me and started patting his pockets for money.

The fiddler gave me a look, right past the three creeps. He stared at me from under these tufty gray eyebrows and jerked his chin the way you point when your hands aren't free: *Get going.*

I got.

Behind me the doors shut and the train roared away into the tunnel toward the next stop.

My knees were so wobbly I almost didn't make it up the stairs to the street.

3

The Fiddler in the Park

Mom was on the warpath again, so I didn't bother her with any of this. I probably wouldn't have anyway. I wouldn't have known how to tell her what had happened.

Anyway, there she was with her new lawyer in the fight against the landlord. They were going over our apartment, making lists of the missing stuff (which now included all the plugs off the ends of the electric cords). If it had been a movie, the lawyer would have been some handsome, upscale type for my mother to fall in love with. Then she'd get married, and all my weird problems would disappear because what I really needed was a father, right?

Actually the lawyer was this carroty-colored woman with an excitable voice. She and Mom were deep in that fast, bright kind of conversation that meant they were on the same wavelength and were going to be friends.

I went into my room and shut the door and walked around in circles, telling myself I was not crazy.

I kept seeing this subway violinist very clearly in my mind: thick gray curly hair and a squarish, calm sort of face, with nests of lines around his mouth and deep sprays of them at the outside corners of his eyes. Funny eyes, with an Oriental slant, but light-colored and bright and watchful, like a cat's. He hadn't looked grubby, like most beggars, but very neat in a rust brown corduroy jacket and pants and a light blue shirt without a tie.

And he had played and we had danced. It was the craziest thing.

But what was it that I had that the Princes of Darkness wanted?

I got very tired, and next thing I knew my mom was waking me up. She asked if I was all right because it was unlike me to sleep in the daytime, and here it was time for dinner.

At the table Mom started in with carefully casual remarks about this guy she'd been out with the night before. That meant I didn't have to listen yet. She wasn't nearly at the point of talking about how I should meet him, how I would like him, how we could all go to a movie together or whatever. At least this one was some kind of senior editor, not a pediatrician like the last one she'd brought around. (I knew a kid once whose uncle was a pediatrician, which meant she got any kind of shot or vaccination that became available, sometimes even before it was available, and that's no way to live.)

When I got that much, I put the conversation on automatic pilot and concentrated on my own problems. Mostly I decided that the subway dance had to have been a hallucination. Maybe Margie wasn't as cubed as she made out. Maybe she had slipped me something in that ginger ale I had at her place.

But I'd tried a couple of pills and things with Megan when she was raiding her mom's medicine cabinet, and I knew what that stuff felt like. Not like this. There never was a pill or anything else that could make me know how to dance.

Maybe I was getting a brain tumor like the boy in *Death Be Not Proud,* and I had imagined the dancing. Maybe I would never get to be introduced to Ralph or Howard or whatever the editor's name was, because I would be a vegetable by morning.

I fell asleep sweaty with terror and trying to find the headache I'd had the day before, to sort of get the feel of it and see if it felt like a tumor, if that's what a tumor feels like.

The next day I coasted through school as if there was a plate glass door between me and everybody else. I tried, once, to talk to Megan about what had happened. All she was interested in was what the three Princes had looked like. She made moronic jokes about how I'd have been better off with them than with some grubby old pervert, meaning I should watch out for the man with the violin, not the creeps. She even got a laugh out of me, calling him a "molester." I couldn't help it.

This was a joke from when we saw the words *child molester* once in the paper and were struck by the obvious pronunciation. Girls in New York have to get wise about sickies pretty young. You either learn to see them coming a long way off and get out of the way fast or you give up ever going outside.

"I'm too old to be mole-sted," I said, and Megan said, "You're never too old, thank goodness. Now, when Micky tries to mole-st me . . ."

Off she went again. I made a joke about "Micky Mole-ster," and she got furious and stomped off. There just wasn't any point in talking to Megan anymore.

My heart sort of lurched with joy when I heard faint violin music as I headed into the park to go home that afternoon. A little group of people were gathered around a man playing his fiddle on Jagiello's terrace.

As I hurried over he finished, and people dropped money into the open violin case on the ground and wandered off, all except a skinny boy in chinos and a checked shirt and a scarf around his neck, who was sitting on the rock by the lake. He wasn't from my school or my building. I didn't know him, but at least he didn't wear a gray nylon jacket. I felt safe in ignoring him. It was the violinist I needed to talk to.

He was squatting by the open violin case, fishing out the money. Boy, what would people have given him if they'd seen the Princes of Darkness dancing to his tune? I felt like that was my secret I shared with him (and the rotten Princes, of course, assuming they even knew what had happened), and that gave me the nerve to walk right up and talk to him.

"Hi," I said.

"Hello," he said. He had a slow voice with a foreign touch to it, and he sounded surprised and pleased to see me. He carefully set the instrument and the bow into the case's blue velvet lining and draped a square of bright colored silk over them.

"Thanks for helping," I said. "Yesterday. In the sub-way."

"Good thing you got in touch," he said. He definitely had an accent. "We knew there was something wrong, but we didn't know where."

Now, the funny thing was I didn't have a clue as to what he was talking about, but I had this perfectly sure feeling that it would all make sense pretty soon. I also knew I was in something weird up to my neck, enough to make my hair prickle when I thought of the three Princes, and it made me feel a lot better to be here talking to this guy with the violin. Because he knew something. And he was going to tell me, as if I were another human being, not just a kid that you don't tell anything to until it's all over.

I knew this because as soon as we sat down together on the low wall that rims the terrace on three sides, he pulled a beat-up package of cigarettes out of his jacket pocket and offered me one. No big deal, he just held out the pack with this inquiring look.

I've tried smoking. My throat closes up and I gag. It's very inelegant, and I could tell from his clothes—everything worn and a little frayed but fadedly clean and pressed into sharp edges, socks and shoes almost the same rust brown as his corduroy suit—that this was a very elegant person. But I loved him for making the offer.

I smiled and shook my head, and he said, "You mind?" And I said no, so he lit a smoke for himself and stuck the cigarette in the corner of his mouth and looked at me, squinting past the smoke and a swipe of his hair that curled down his forehead on one side.

"I didn't know I got in touch," I said. "How did I do that?"

"The way your granny taught you," he said.

Make a wish by running water and seal it with silver.

"Oh shit," I said—I didn't mean to; it just jumped out of me, and I had this ripply feeling of mixed-up delight and terror inside—"you must be from Sorcery Hall!"

See, when I was little, Granny Gran used to do sort of magic things. She could find anything I had lost and tell me what I was getting for my birthday and heal up my canary when it was walking in the hall one afternoon and Mom didn't see it and accidentally stepped on it and semi-squished it (which she said was the canary's fault because it was a bird and was supposed to be flying, not walking around in the dark hall). Whenever I asked Granny Gran how she did those things, she'd say, "Oh, it's something I learned in Sorcery Hall."

That's why I said, "You must be from Sorcery Hall!"

The violinist just nodded and blew smoke out of his nose.

I said, "Are you looking for my Granny Gran? She's in New Jersey."

He shook his head. "I don't want to bother her. I'm looking for you."

"Me?"

"You're the one who got in touch."

"Actually," I said, "what I asked for was Jagiello." And there was no way this medium-short, wiry person in corduroy could be that huge, clunky warrior in armor come down magically off his horse to answer me. "I mean," I added, feeling stupid for the way I said it—as if I was rejecting him for not being exactly what I asked for, that is—"you're not him, are you?"

"No," he said. "We'll find out how that works after a while, though."

"Well, what am I, um, supposed to do now?"

"We got to figure that out. What we start with is, I need your help."

News to me. I thought I'd been the one who wished for help. I said, "Help with what?"

"Well, you got a kraken here."

"A what?"

"A kraken."

He'd offered me a cigarette, he was sitting here talking with me like a real person, and he knew my Granny Gran. Looking sideways at him so as not to seem to be staring, I could see he wasn't nearly as old as Granny Gran, but he was old, all right, old enough to be a friend of hers. You know how grown-ups are pretty much just grown-ups, meaning *not young,* whatever their age, when you first look at them? People in a class with your mom, for instance. But then there are the grown-ups who are old people, which I think means they get to the point where they don't bother trying to pretend they're young anymore, so you just take them as they are or leave them, which is a great relief. Usually they have gray hair and they stand up a little more slowly than regular grown-ups, that kind of thing. I decided the violinist was one of those.

That meant to me that, with him, it was okay not to know everything. He wouldn't look down on me for it, the way grown-ups do sometimes for that kind of thing, putting you down for being *too* young.

So I said, "What's a kraken?"

He rubbed at the side of his neck. "Okay. It's a negative interstitial vortex with a big appetite, and it's going to try and eat up your world if we don't stop it."

"Whoa," I said, breathless. "Some kind of a monster?"

"Yah," he said, nodding and blowing smoke.

I looked kind of wildly around me, checking to make sure the park was still there. The skinny boy in chinos was still sitting there, picking at the black rock with a pencil and glancing up in our direction and away again, fast. I wondered if he was some kind of a scout for the Princes, deliberately out of uniform so I wouldn't recognize him.

The violinist must have noticed me looking. "Don't worry about him," he said. "He's all right."

"You know him?" I said.

"No. But he's all right."

"What does a kraken look like?" I said, keeping my voice down.

"Depends. It hasn't formed up here yet, physically. But it will, if it can get in. It's already found a place where your defenses are so weak that it can break through pretty soon."

"I don't get it," I said.

"You got a slip someplace in the system, and this kraken that's been spinning out there no place for a long time sees a chance to break into a nice warm world and eat it up. It happens sometimes. People get a little careless, they don't clean up after their work just right, and you get a fault and a kraken working on it.

"Your own people that knew about these things left all kinds of protection, special barriers and guardians to keep out something like a kraken. You got the pyramids, the great kiva at Chaco Canyon, big ones like that; and then lots of smaller ones. Only when people get into this mechanistic stage you're in right now, they start moving things, tearing them down, breaking them to pieces to make room for something new without knowing what they're doing. It's a risky time for anybody.

"You make enough mistakes, you can weaken the system. You bulldoze this Indian graveyard, you close down that old theater nobody cares about, you rip out a special grove of trees to put in some tract housing—pretty soon you got weakness where you need to have strength.

"Now the kraken is doing its own moving, getting the way completely clear to come in here and chew it all up."

"Jagiello!" I said. "It moved Jagiello!"

He nodded. "Yah. He's the key. This park was made to hold down a local manifestation of the weakness and Jagiello was put here to seal that place. Him, and the little castle there, and what you call Cleopatra's Needle."

Cleopatra's Needle is a stone obelisk from Egypt, which stands on a little hill across the path northward from Jagiello's hill, half hidden by cherry trees.

"But some of those are modern things," I said. "Don't you need really ancient monuments, like Stonehenge?"

"Not Stonehenge," he said, shaking his head. "It's a little out of whack, always was. Avebury, yah. There are plenty of newer things, too. Even when you don't know exactly *why* anymore, there are still people around with a good instinct for where a marker or a guardian is needed, and they put it there and say it looks pretty.

"Trouble here is, they took the weather instruments off the castle roof, which was a mistake; and the hiero-glyphs that give the needle its power are almost worn off by erosion. With two down, it wasn't so hard for the kraken to shove the third out of the way. So those three that stood guard here are disarmed or lost.

"Which doesn't have to mean something terrible, provided we can find Jagiello and get him back in position in the next few days. I can go around and fiddle up the power of some other markers you got around here, and with them he can hold the line all right. Only we got to find him."

This stranger was going to want something from me after all. I felt disappointed, as though I'd let somebody put something over on me. Maybe he was just a nut, a fancy nut with a great imagination and a violin.

Except he knew my Granny Gran. So I couldn't just duck out on him. On the other hand, I was not really de-lighted by the idea of being loaded with more stuff to do. I mean, with a working mother and me the only child, I already had my hands full a lot of the time. "What have I got to do with any of that?" I said.

"You're mixed up in it somehow," he said, shoving the hair off his forehead and blowing more smoke. "Or what do the Princes want with you? They belong to the kraken."

"You mean they're—magical? Devils or something?" I squeaked.

"No, just creeps, like you call them. They were down in the subway, looking for what they could take off the poor bums who sometimes crawl down there to sleep when it's cold. And they've done worse than just stealing; you don't need to know. The kraken was naturally drawn to them, and it took them on. There are always people dumb enough to agree to that kind of thing."

The Princes! It was way too late to get curious, I realized. With the Princes after me, I was in this anyway, like it or not. I said, "I don't know what they were looking for, but if you hadn't come along and—and—" And what? I didn't know what to say.

He didn't smile, exactly, but the corners of his mouth twitched. "You liked that? Pretty good, eh?"

"How did you do it?"

"I just played good music," he said. He was sort of twinkling at me, but still, well, *serious*. It was weird, in a warm sort of way. His light gray eyes looked right at me the whole time we talked, right into my eyes, which was actually uncomfortable for me. I knew his stare was friendly, wasn't a stare at all really. It was just his way of looking at a person. But I had to keep looking away.

He said, "What are you called?"

Which surprised me—you'd think a magician would know your name. "Tina," I said.

He shook his head. "No," he said.

"No what?" I said. "Tina, that's my name—for Valentine. Mr., ah—?"

He said something that sounded like "Povvo," only the first syllable was pronounced more like the *a* in "cat" than like *o*.

"Um, could you spell that for me, Mr. Povvo?" I said.

"P-a-a-v-o," he said. "And it's my first name. The last name is Latvela, but call me Paavo, okay? We don't need formal for what we got to do."

He stuck out his hand and we shook. He didn't have the kind of hands you'd expect in a musician, all slim and arty-looking. My hand got squeezed in this thick, warm, meaty mitt.

I said, "Can you tell me why things are disappearing?"

Thank goodness, for once I didn't have to explain or convince or anything. He said, "You mean besides Jagiello?"

"Yes, like our linoleum and my sandwich and—"

"Tell me the whole list," he said.

I did. He listened without saying anything, just taking a puff on his cigarette every now and then and squinting past the smoke.

Then he said, "The kraken is trying to get from you whatever it is you got that it wants. The Princes are one way to get it from you. The kraken is using other ways, too. Only it can't get a good fix on this thing, whatever it is, so it's grabbing around blind for anything it senses might be connected with you."

"Will the lost things ever get found again?" I said. I mean, who knew what else was gone besides what I was personally aware of? Who knew what else might go? My mother was connected with me, for one thing. You can fight all you want with your mom, but you don't want to have to try and get along without one altogether. Also I wanted my sneakers back.

Paavo shrugged. "Maybe. I'd like my cap back, too."

"It's gone?" I said. "You think the kraken took it?"

"No, I think somebody grabbed it while I was sleeping last night, but I don't know for sure. It's okay, it was a little too small anyhow."

I wondered where he had slept where he could have his stuff stolen; not outside, I hoped, but there was no point in asking because there was nothing I could do about it if that was where he slept. I asked instead about what was really on my mind.

"What can we do about this kraken?"

"Nothing today," he said, glancing up at the sky. "The air's all wrong and the light's bad." It was true we had this low overcast, very gray and dimming.

"You said we only have a few days!"

"Yah. Meet me here tomorrow, same time. We'll see if we can find Jagiello." He got up and took his violin case and walked away, just like that.

He wasn't tall but he walked with his head up, as though he was looking somebody taller right in the eye, and he had a quick, precise step that reminded me of some very sure-footed, bright-eyed animal—maybe a mountain goat. I thought he was neat.

On my way home I stopped outside the local deli, the Lox Populi, where I shop a lot for Mom. Mr. Canetti and Mr. Steinberg, the owners, were out on the sidewalk with a bunch of cops. The two old guys were stamping and yelling and waving their arms.

"Next time it could be the whole building!" Mr. Canetti shouted. "And who sees anything, who hears, who knows? Where are the police? Out giving tickets! While some lousy bums are carrying out a whole goddamn cold case loaded with food!"

"Take it easy, Frank," Mr. Steinberg said. "You'll have a heart attack." Then he took over the yelling while Mr. Canetti stood there glaring around like an old walrus.

Somebody behind me said, "What's going on?"

It was the skinny boy from the park.

4

Fiddle Magic

Paavo had said this kid was all right, so he must be all right. In fact he was nice-looking, in a sharp-faced, irritable way, with long reddish brown hair and a green scarf tied around his neck. Now that I thought of it, I might have seen him before in the neighborhood. "Do you live around here?"

"No, on the East Side, but I've got friends over here. Why are those old guys in such an uproar?"

"Somebody stole their cold case," I said. "Full of food."

He said, "Who, King Kong?"

I laughed, and we hung around and talked a little, pointing out to each other the cop who kept picking his nose and the one with the ketchup on his shirt, that kind of thing. He said what about some coffee or soda or whatever, and I said fine, and we ended up in a coffee shop on Broadway where I finally found out what he was after.

His name was Joel Wechsler. I liked his sort of cranky hawk looks and his bright scarf and his nervous, long-fingered hands that kept torturing the rim of his wax-coated paper Coke cup all the time we talked.

He asked about Paavo.

"Has he been playing there long, your friend the fiddler?" he said.

"No," I said, getting cautious. Paavo was one heck of a big secret, after all, him and Sorcery Hall and the kraken, and who knew how much this kid had managed to overhear? I began to wish Paavo hadn't gone off and left me with this situation. I began to mentally limber up my I-have-to-go-home-now speech.

"I didn't think I'd seen him there before," he said. "Most of these guys have fixed beats, you know? A kind of informal territory. Maybe he's just started trying it out there, though I don't think anybody could make much of a living playing on weekdays in Central Park."

"He can," I said, knowing nothing at all about what I was talking about. "He's good."

Joel hunched over the Coke cup, peeling the wax out of the rolled rim. "Well, he sounds all right, even on that beat-up old fiddle. But if he was really good he'd be playing in an orchestra, wouldn't he? Or in a chamber group, or he'd even be an international soloist. Maybe he just had a good day today, who knows?"

"Listen," I said, getting up, "I've got to go home now."

He scowled up at me. "Is he a friend of your family's or something?"

"I only met him today," I said, and I headed for the door. I was feeling kind of funny, too, sort of annoyed that this boy really didn't want to talk to me at all. He just wanted to pump me about Paavo.

He dropped some money on the table and came after me. "Didn't your mother ever tell you not to talk to strangers?" he said, following me out onto the street.

"That's right," I said, "and you're a stranger, so I guess I better not talk to you."

"Hey, I'm sorry if I said the wrong thing," he said, keeping up, which wasn't hard considering that he was a foot taller than I was. "But you should be careful in this town."

"I know that," I said. "I was born here."

"Me, too," he said. He swung along next to me with his hands in his pockets, staring at the sidewalk. "I always wanted to live in the country, but my father . . ."

"Your father what?"

"He needs to be here for his work."

Funny having your dad around, and having to live where his work was. I looked at Joel curiously. He didn't look very cheerful.

When we stopped at my building, Joel said, "You live here?"

"Yes," I said, standing there feeling half-impatient to get away from him and half-hoping he would stay and talk some more (but not about Paavo). I wouldn't have minded if some of the kids in the building should happen to see me out here talking to this interesting, though not particularly sunny-natured, stranger. He was really very nice-looking, if only he would smile.

"I used to know a very fine pianist who lived here," he said.

I was surprised. "You mean Mr. Vishinsky? I remember him. I used to hear him playing when I went to sleep at night. The music came right down through the whole courtyard. I was sorry when he died."

I didn't know anything about classical music except that a lot of it really got to me, and that was partly due to that ghostly music drifting down the air shaft from Mr. Vishinsky's open window.

"He didn't just die," Joel said. "He killed himself."

"Oh," I said.

"Anyway, that's what I heard," he went on, staring past me into the lobby. "Because it wasn't ever going to come back."

"What wasn't?"

"The control in his left hand. Why do you think he quit concertizing? He got that creeping nerve disease pianists get sometimes. You lost the strength, the control you need."

"God, how awful. I always thought his music sounded wonderful." Joel gave me this sour look that said as plain as words, shows how much you know. "Well, I don't know much about good music. I only hear what my mom plays on the stereo."

"If you'd heard Vishinsky live, when he was still okay, you'd know the difference," he said, "probably."

"How did you know him? Did you take piano lessons with him?" Mr. Vishinsky had had lots of students.

"My father knew him." Joel shifted his weight again, looking up the block. I thought, he doesn't like me, he wants to be someplace else. He said, "So is he going to be there again tomorrow?"

"Who?" I said.

"Your pal, the fiddler?"

"I don't know," I lied. I decided on the spot that I would rather fall dead where I stood than have Joel Wechsler show up in the park tomorrow when Paavo and I took on the kraken. "No," I added, "come to think of it, no, he isn't. He told me it wasn't working out as well as he thought, so he was going to try someplace else."

Joel looked hard at me. "Did he say where?"

"Someplace downtown, one of the other parks."

"The other parks are mainly full of junkies," he said.

"So?" I said. "Maybe he buys from the dealers, how would I know? Aren't musicians all dopers anyway?"

Joel made a contemptuous grunt and walked away, his hands still in his pockets.

"Thanks for the soda," I yelled after him. "Creep." But that, of course, I kept under my breath.

I went upstairs and stood at my window for a long time, wondering if Joel or Paavo or the Princes or even the kraken would show up down there on the sidewalk. Eventually I wrote a little in my diary about Joel and a lot more about Paavo, and then I actually got some homework done.

This turned out to be a good thing, because that evening was not very productive for work. At eight o'clock the landlord came barging into the apartment to accuse my mother of vandalizing his building for deep, dark reasons of her own. All the mail chutes had disappeared, leaving long, pale strips down the walls of the hallways across from the elevators. We were also to blame for the stuff missing from our apartment. The landlord called my mom an "urban communist cadre."

My mother called her lawyer.

I took my homework into the bathroom and thought about various ways to tell my mother and the lawyer and the landlord that the disappearances were really about something I had that I didn't know I had that a kraken wanted.

That was also the night, according to the next day's news, on which the famed Sabatini string quartet played their final concert of a series in Carnegie Hall, but due to what the papers called an "accoustical freak," nobody could hear a sound. The musicians said they heard their own music just fine. Everybody else sat there thinking they themselves had gone crazy or deaf.

This news report scared me. Maybe the kraken *had* taken Paavo's cap. Maybe the kraken was onto Paavo through me, and was trying to grab him now by grabbing at music, the kind of music Paavo played. Maybe the next thing connected with me that would disappear would be Paavo himself. Then I'd be out there alone with this secret that I barely understood and nobody to help, even if they knew how to.

Some things happened in school the next day, but I have no memory of what they were. The only thing I was interested in was looking up "kraken" in the library. The dictionary said the word is from a Norwegian dialect and that it means "fabulous Scandinavian sea monster."

Great. Norwegian fairy tales. But Paavo hadn't sounded like a Scandinavian to me.

He was from someplace a lot farther away than that. He knew my grandmother and he came from Sorcery Hall.

As soon as I got out of social studies class I grabbed my books and stuff and ran for the park. I looked around to see if Joel was lurking someplace, didn't see him, and was glad. I did not want him sticking his nose into whatever this was I had to do with Paavo.

On the terrace at the east end of the lake, Paavo was playing. There was a crowd, not big but respectable. I thought the music sounded good, very rich and strong.

And there was Joel, sitting on the side wall with his chin on his hands. I went over to him.

"Will you go away?" I said. "I can take care of myself!"

Joel glared. "Be quiet, I'm listening!"

The music wound up with a singing flourish, and the people applauded and stood around for a little bit. A man shook Paavo's hand, started talking to him, and handed him some cash. So I guess it really was good music. I felt proud because Paavo was my friend.

He came toward us, holding his violin by the neck with the same hand he held the bow in: so practiced and casual-looking.

"Hi," I said, ignoring the fact that Joel was sitting there.

"Hello," said Paavo.

"My name's Joel," said Joel, before I could say another word. Paavo nodded. Joel said, "Can I ask who you studied with?"

"A lot of people, here and there," Paavo said. From anybody else it would have been a vague answer, but there was nothing vague about him. His gray eyes were sharp and steady on Joel the way they'd been steady on me the day before. "What about you?"

Joel turned pink and put his hand up to his neck where he was wearing another scarf today, a red one. "I don't," he said. "I'm not a string player."

"Then what?" Paavo said.

Turning as red as his scarf now, Joel mumbled, "Lead guitar in a group, that's all. It's just a hobby."

"You do your own compositions?" Paavo said. He dug around in his pockets. I thought, he's going to pull out his cigarettes and offer one to Joel and the two of them will stand around smoking and talking music together and I'm going to cry. I couldn't say a word. I was thinking about just walking away, since nobody seemed to be interested in my being there.

Joel said, "A couple of the other guys are strong on composition. I just play, man."

Paavo nodded. What he brought out of his pocket was a lump of chalk. "Okay, you ready?"

He was talking to me. Feeling ignored and not ready to help out, I said, "Uh, what for?"

"To find Jagiello. Joel, can you get up there on that marble block where the statue used to stand?"

"Sure," Joel said. I had been hoping that he would ask a question, get an answer that wouldn't make any sense to him, and take off, or better yet, be sent off by Paavo. But Joel was smart. He didn't ask anything, he just started showing off. He tried to chin himself up onto Jagiello's plinth. It was too high. Paavo put his violin down gently. He walked over and grabbed Joel's foot and gave him a leg up. Joel was taller than Paavo, but Paavo was strong, which made me feel proud of Paavo. I guess because Joel was such a smart ass, though not when he was face to face with Paavo I noticed.

"Okay," Paavo said, dusting his palms together and looking up at Joel. "Now come stand at the front, that's right."

"Am I supposed to be able to see the statue from up here?" Joel said.

"No. Just stand there. Good."

Paavo lit a cigarette, sank onto his haunches, and began drawing with the chalk on the pavement. I hovered. He was humming. What he drew was an outline. It was a funny, lumpy shape, sort of oblong and aimed at the lake.

"What's that?" I said.

Paavo drew these two crossed shapes at one end and I knew. It was an outline of the shadow of the King's statue, except that there was no shadow on the ground but Joel's, inside the outline.

"What about the Princes?" I said. "What if they come?"

"They won't," he said. "I gave them some things to do." He hummed some more, and I knew without being told that when he was doing that, I'd better not speak to him. I could see how he was concentrating. His hair stuck to his forehead because he was sweating with concentration.

"Okay," he said, sitting back on his heels. "You can come down."

Joel swung himself down. "What now?" he said, very manly, ready for anything.

Paavo pocketed the chalk, stood, and tucked his violin under his chin. "I'll play. You sing, Val. Joel will write down the words."

"I can't sing," I said, panicking. I mean, God, out there in the open and in front of Joel and Paavo both?

"Sha," Paavo said. "It's not the opera. Don't worry."

"But I can't—there are people—"

"Don't worry," he said. "Stand here, inside the chalk line. No, face the lake, like the statue did."

I did. I could see the rising tiers of seats inside the Delacorte Theatre at the other end of the lake, and the trees, and then on the left the black crag with the little castle on top of it. I could see some mommies and little kids sitting on the grass on the north side of the lake with their baby carriages. Maybe if I sang very softly they wouldn't hear me.

Paavo stood behind me. I couldn't see Joel either. I started to sing, What's the song? What am I supposed to be singing? But the violin sounded and everything left my mind. My whole skin sort of prickled and shivered and settled quietly again, and I could hear exactly what the violin said. It said, in rich string tones, *Oh Defender, your place is empty. We seek you. Where are you?*

I opened my mouth and out of my throat something like a cool wind came rushing. I heard a huge, hollow voice ringing all through my head. I couldn't understand a single word. It sounded like total gibberish. My cheeks got hot, and I had to shut my eyes.

Paavo laughed a real guffaw. "Okay," he said, "that's a start, anyhow."

"What?" Joel said. "I didn't get a word."

"It's Korean for 'I can't take a picture of you from here; there's a tree growing out of your ear.' Your King Jagiello's only a statue. He's got nothing much in his head, you know? He only knows what he's heard people say around him. But he hears us and he's answering. Let's try again."

"You know Korean?" Joel said, sounding outraged and hopeless. But Paavo was playing again, the same question: *Where are you?*

I heard this same big metal voice come out of my throat: "What shrill-voiced suppliant makes this eager cry?"

"Ah," said Paavo. "Joel, pay attention. Write down everything Val says."

The violin sang, *I am a friend, an adept, and your Master. Where are you, Defender?*

And I answered, or the big voice answered, anyhow, "This palace of dim night . . . When I was at home, I was in a better place."

How were you taken from that home?

"Imprisoned in the viewless winds, and blown with restless violence round about the pendant world."

Oh, oh. "Round the world" sounded pretty serious. What if Jagiello was in China? And who in the world had been hanging around Jagiello's statue talking like this?

Paavo's violin sang, *Defender, what do you see?*

I myself saw small ripples on the brownish surface of the lake, spreading from where one of the little kids was stirring the water with a stick. The huge voice poured out of me and all around me, the voice nobody else seemed to hear: "Night and silence . . . Out went the candle, and we were left darkling . . . Hung be the heavens with black, yield day to night!"

What do you feel?

"Are you not mov'd when all the sway of earth shakes like a thing infirm?"

I hoped Paavo could make something out of all this because I sure couldn't. I felt stupid, being in the middle of whatever was going on but left out at the same time because I didn't understand it.

Paavo played, *What do you hear?*

"This dreadful night that thunders, lightens, opens graves, roars as doth the lion in the Capitol."

Ha! Jagiello was talking Shakespeare! I'd read *Julius Caesar* in English class, and "the lion in the Capitol" is part of somebody's speech about the terrible storm that happens the night before Caesar gets killed. Jagiello was putting his answers together with the words he'd soaked up from the plays performed every summer in the open-air theater at the other end of the lake. I started to giggle.

The great voice pushed right on through me: "To the dread rattling thunder have I given fire . . . and rifted Jove's stout oak with his own bolt . . . the strong-based promontory have I made shake . . . and by the spurs pluck'd up the pine and cedar . . . graves at my command have waked their sleepers, oped, and let them forth by my so potent art."

Graves again. I was completely baffled. Where could he be?

Especially when almost as an afterthought the huge voice added, "The rabblement hooted . . . I heard a bustling rumor like a fray."

First silence, and then roaring noise, and someplace in there he could hear voices? I was as confused as ever and getting tired.

And what scents the air about you? sang the violin. Which struck me as a funny question to a statue that had a solid bronze nose that no scent could possibly get into. It crossed my mind that I was completely nuts and hallucinating and probably actually in a mental ward someplace, just a poor cuckoo case like whatsername who wrote that book *I Never Promised You a Rose Garden.*

"The fire and cracks of sulphurous roaring—"

Then there came this horrendous blast of noise like a hurricane. I reeled out of the chalk outline and crashed down on the pavement, with my palms stinging from the impact.

The noise came from the boom box that Tattoo had brought up behind us and turned on full blast. The three Princes had sneaked up on us in plain sight, in the park, and they had us surrounded.

5

Mugged

Joel dropped the book he'd been writing in and jumped up, but the Princes moved fast and they ignored him and me completely. They closed in around Paavo, and there was a quick, heaving kind of struggle. Then Pins-and-Grins stepped back, holding Paavo's violin high in the air.

That stopped Joel in his tracks, his eyes on the instrument. Tattoo and the Chewer had Paavo's arms clamped behind his back.

The whole thing happened so fast it paralyzed me. I gaped.

Pins-and-Grins said, "You make any money playing today, old man? We're just poor students, we wouldn't mind if you'd sort of help us out."

"Hey," Joel said. What was he waiting for? I started to get up, though what I was going to do I didn't know. The suddenness, the violence so close and so fast has sort of shocked me flat, the way it can do if you're not used to that kind of thing. I had this slow, sluggish feeling in my arms and legs so that it was all of a sudden a huge production to get up off the pavement.

"Let him go!" Joel said loudly. Maybe he had the same heaviness on him that I had, maybe he couldn't move?

49

Or maybe he was plain scared. There were three of them, and they were bigger than he was except for Tattoo, who looked strong in that ropy way that small, skinny guys can be strong.

Paavo stood braced back in their grip. He looked awful—yellow in the face and blank like someone who'd been yanked out of a deep sleep.

"Not making out so good, eh?" Pins sneered. He looked at the violin. "What about this? Maybe it's a priceless Stradivarius or something?"

"Hell no," Tattoo crowed. "It's a piece of junk, man! All he can get out of it is those weird noises we heard."

"Oh, well, if it's just a piece of junk," Pins said, and he turned and swung it hard against the edge of the pink marble plinth where Jagiello used to stand. The instrument exploded into fragments. Shards of wood hung from the scroll by the strings.

"Oops," said Pins, right over a raw, deep gasp from Paavo. "Look what happened. But the way it sounded, I figured we just did you a favor, you know?"

Joel flung himself on Pins. With a lot of grunting and scrabbling the two of them went down. Tattoo let go of Paavo and danced around them, looking for a chance to clobber Joel with that huge radio of his.

Paavo, with the Chewer holding one of his arms twisted behind him, threw back his head and let out this terrible cry that made me go all lurchy inside.

But then I heard something else—a siren, a police siren! One of the police cars that patrol the park must be coming! Someone had reported something. We were going to be saved!

Tattoo hugged his blaster to his chest and took off, hollering back over his shoulder, "Come on, let's go!" Pins-and-Grins whomped Joel in the stomach and scrambled up. The Chewer gave Paavo a shove that sent him staggering. Then he and Pins-and-Grins careened out of the park after Tattoo, laughing and whooping as if it had all been a great game.

The sirens got louder and nearer and seemed to pass by us, following the Princes, and then they died away. Where were the police cars?

I climbed to my feet, all gulpy with shock.

The mommies were still sitting on the grass, and the kids were playing at the edge of the water. Nobody else had been flattened and battered but us three, nobody else had heard sirens.

Paavo had done it.

He stood sort of holding himself up on one of the lacy antique lampposts on the terrace. I felt terrible, and I was angry. At him. What kind of a wizard lets himself get roughed up like that by a bunch of creeps, anyway? I couldn't stand looking at Paavo and being sorry for him.

He spat out a word: "*Perkele!*"

"What?" I said.

"It means 'damn,'" he said harshly.

"In Korean?" I was really half out of it, that's all I can say in my defense.

"In Finn."

"Oh."

"Ugh," he said. He let go of the lamppost and worked his shoulders as if they ached. "Everybody okay?"

"I'm fine, I'm fine," I said. "But you said they wouldn't come. What happened?"

He looked bitterly disgusted. "I got careless. *Damn* it. I thought I had them all fixed, I gave them plenty to do. I been going around the city today, playing some strength back into some of the markers and guardians they been fooling with. The kraken's had them neutralizing all kinds of things. I thought if I put most of it right, they'd be sent out again with the spray can, hammers, and pliers—some of your markers are pretty easy to wreck. It doesn't take much, it doesn't take long, not as long as to fix it again. But long enough, I thought. I was wrong. The kraken has a stronghold here already."

He coughed.

"Are you all right?" I said. Maybe they'd really hurt him. I felt scared and furious.

"Tired," he said. "They didn't do me any real damage personally. But it's always bad to get interrupted like that in the middle of things. Also I think I did too much this morning. I'm not used to conditions here. My conditions." He looked down at his hands and flexed his fingers. "I should have waited." He bent over like an old man, I mean a really old man, picked up the bow he'd been using, and sat down on the wall, shaking his head. "Too impatient, too quick, always the same thing. Damn. If I wasn't already tired out from this morning's work, I'd have felt them coming, I wouldn't have let them catch me like that. I'd have been faster when they moved in, I might have stopped them. Shaa." He shoved one hand through his hair and looked at us. "You sure you're both all right?"

Joel nodded. His lips looked white. He got up carefully. He still didn't ask anything. I would have admired him for that, except that I was so upset. So I did what you do when you're upset, I guess. I turned on him.

"God, Joel, why didn't you jump in sooner? If only you'd done something right away—"

Ignoring me, he walked over, limping a little, and looked down at the smashed violin. Then he stood in front of Paavo, who was fumbling around with his cigarettes.

"Look," Joel said in this low, trembly voice, "I'm sorry. If I'd realized—"

Paavo inhaled and blew smoke through his nostrils. "Realized what?" he said. "You still don't really believe even what you saw, do you? Don't apologize, you did fine. I'm the only one who knows all about what goes on here, so I'm the only one to blame, okay? And I don't like blame, so I better do something to fix it, yah? First thing, let's see what we got before the Princes came."

We looked for Joel's history text. He'd been taking Jagiello's dictation on the inside back cover. The book was gone. The Princes must have gotten it.

"Shakespeare," I said. "It was Shakespeare and it was all about darkness and roaring and stuff."

"Yes, but that's not exact enough," Paavo said. "If we could just try a little more—" You could see him stiffening against the impulse to turn toward the ruined violin.

"Listen," Joel said. "Maybe I can do something, um, I mean there's a possibility—I don't know exactly what you were—what we were doing, what you were playing just now. But could you take up where we left off if you had another fiddle?"

Paavo looked at his bow. "Well," he said, "maybe we could do something, I don't know how much. There's no time to do the job right." Now he did glance over at the smashed violin and quickly away again. I knew without being told that he'd worked with it for years, filling it with magic one thin layer at a time.

"Still, with a decent instrument, maybe we could do something tomorrow. Today is shot anyhow. But a good fiddle is expensive, isn't it? I don't have a bank account. I didn't know to fix that up. You got something in mind?"

Joel said, "Let's go to my house. I think I have something there you could use."

Paavo nodded and got up. He took the smashed remains of the old violin, laid them gently in the battered black case, and went to the edge of the water. I didn't watch what he did—it had made me feel terrible to see how lovingly he'd handled the broken bits—but I think he sank the case and the wreckage in the lake.

He rejoined us with just his bow in his hand. We trudged out of the park to the East Side and got a cab. Joel said he had money. We headed uptown.

Paavo sat in the middle of the back seat. He didn't smoke, maybe because the cab had a sign in it, "This is my home. I don't come fill your living room with smoke and butts and ashes." Something like that.

Joel was rubbing his left hand, stretching the fingers out and pulling on them gingerly.

"Let's see your hand," Paavo said.

He took Joel's hand and felt it all over and even reached up under Joel's sleeve a little. "What did you do, punch him?"

Joel nodded, looking miserable and mad.

"Next time bite. Kick, use your knees, your skull. They're harder and stronger than hands. Anyhow, you just bruised yourself a little, you'll be okay."

"For the guitar, maybe," Joel said. "What about playing the violin?"

"I thought you didn't play," Paavo said.

"I don't, not anymore," Joel muttered, looking at the floor of the cab. "I mean I used to, but I quit. I'm thinking of going back to it again."

"No real problem with the hand," Paavo said. "How long since you played?"

"A few years."

Paavo thought. He said, "Depends what you want to do. A concert career, solo performance—you've lost some time."

"I know that," Joel snapped. "I didn't say I *was* going back. I said I was thinking about it. Right on this corner is fine," he told the driver, and we piled out in front of a superluxury apartment building on Park Avenue.

"Mmm," said Paavo. "Nice."

We went in. The man at the desk in the lobby gave us this look.

"It's okay, Barney," Joel said. "This is Tina, from my school, and this is a friend, a violinist."

"Somebody jump you or something?" Barney said to him, squinting suspiciously at Paavo. "You want me to try and reach your mother?"

"No, it's okay. I had a little trouble in the park, but it's not as bad as it looks. I'll tell my parents myself later. I wouldn't want to scare anybody."

In the elevator the uniformed guy who punched the button for us said, "Mrs. Rouse isn't there right now, Joel."

"It's okay, I've got my keys," Joel said.

We went down the hall with the elevator man's eyes drilling us through the back. "Who's Mrs. Rouse?" I whispered.

"Housekeeper," Joel said. He unlocked the door.

Well, I could see why they needed a housekeeper; there was a lot of house to keep. We walked into this enormous, bright apartment, lit by a huge window on an outside terrace. There was a lot of pale, polished wood everywhere, a lot of wall space, and a few hangings and prints full of exotic colors and designs. A jungle of potted plants crowded around the big window and spilled out onto the terrace beyond.

The living room had to be big. There was a grand piano in it. A bunch of music stands, like a little crowd of silver stick figures, stood nearby with a few chairs among them.

"Holy cow," I said.

Joel said, "I'll go and see if there's anything to nosh on in the kitchen."

He went.

Paavo walked over to the big window and sank down into a sofa facing it, looking out. I had a feeling he needed not to have anybody close by for a little while, so I sort of drifted around the room looking at things: books, shelves of music scores for chamber groups mostly, some photos on the wall.

One of them was of a kid I thought was Joel, but younger. He was standing on a stage with his arms lifted, and a bunch of musicians were poised in front of him to play.

Now I knew: Richard Wechsler, of course, the prodigy. He was conducting whole orchestras even though he was only about twelve. A genius, they said.

"Hey, Joel," I said, sticking my head in the kitchen. "Is Richard Wechsler your brother?"

He was putting cookies on a plate. "That's right," he said. "And Abraham Wechsler is my father. He plays the cello. My mom's a singer, but you might not know her name, not unless you're an opera freak. Are you?"

"No," I said. I was getting the picture, all right.

He said, "You want to take these out there? If he wants tea or coffee, there's instant in the cupboard, and I've got water heating in that pot."

"Where are you going?" I said.

"To get him a violin."

6
Tea and Cookies

Paavo ate up all the cookies and drank some tea full of sugar. Then he turned to the violin that lay gleaming in an open case on the sofa where Joel had put it.

Paavo touched his bow to the strings, tightened up two pegs, and played a few notes. I don't know what that music was, but in one instant I felt as if I was hovering in space someplace, on the verge of dissolving in some huge wave of feeling that would pass and leave me never the same.

Then the music turned all thoughtful and slow and beyond me. I mean I could hear how beautiful it was, but I couldn't follow it exactly. Nothing stayed in my head in the way of a tune or anything with a shape.

Collapsed next to me in a big old chair, Joel groaned.

"Well," he said when the music stopped, "I guess there's nothing left but suicide."

Paavo said, "Shaa. Coming from a family with all that talent, you'll do fine."

"I don't care about 'fine,'" Joel said angrily. "Anybody can do 'fine.'"

"Yah?" Paavo said, sounding interested. "Anybody? Val, here, if she wanted?"

"I didn't mean that," Joel said.

58

"No," Paavo said.

"I meant—" Joel stared at the floor. "You can't just lope along in the concert world, you know? It's all or nothing. Either you've got it, or you end up fifth chair in some lousy community orchestra in Podunk. Or on the street, fiddling for pennies."

I gasped. I mean, that was an incredibly crass thing to say, considering Paavo's circumstances. Joel pushed on, sounding fierce. "That can happen even to good players. I know. Anything can happen. You don't even want to start unless you've got all the cards already stacked in your hand."

Suddenly he leaned forward and said, "Teach me. I don't know what's going on, who you are, anything, but I'll help, I'll do whatever you want and not ask a single question—only teach me to play like that!"

I felt stabbed in the heart. Joel was trying to grab the only real wizard in the world for himself, and maybe since they were both musicians, he could. I was just someone who wrote poems sometimes in her journal that she didn't show to anybody. My only claim on Paavo was that he knew my Granny Gran. Great. He probably wouldn't even have included me in his magic at all, except for that. I couldn't look at Paavo. Suppose he told Joel yes?

He touched the strings again with the bow and a thread of song came drifting, like music you might hear from another world, eerie and piercing.

"There may be things I can teach you," he said slowly. "There may be time to do it, too. But I can't make any promises. You understand?"

Joel said, "Just say yes, say you will. What's so hard about that? My father will pay anything you like. I know he will, once he's heard you play. I could catch up in no time, I could play the way I always wanted to, if you'll just teach me!"

"Otherwise you won't lend me this violin?" Paavo said.

"I'm not lending," Joel said. "I'm giving. Take it."

Paavo held the violin delicately in his thick hands. "It's a fine instrument," he said. "Somebody put a lot of love in it when it was made. Is it yours to give?"

Joel said, "Teach me. Please."

"Is that the condition?"

Slowly Joel sat back, looking down now. "No," he croaked. "I can only lend it to you, and there is no condition."

"Good," Paavo said. "As long as we know where we are, here. Thanks for the tea and cookies. I'll meet you both again tomorrow."

He put the violin away, hesitated a minute, and then put his own bow in the case with it. Then he shut the case and got up to go. I thought already he looked fresher, stronger than before, as if that little bit of music-making had helped him. He handed Joel the case.

Joel looked at him. "But aren't you going to take it with you?"

"How far would I get with this? He didn't like the look of me, that watchdog downstairs. I came in with only my bow. What will he think if I walk out of here carrying this? No, you keep it for me. Bring it tomorrow. Not to the lake;

they may be watching for us there now. In the little park by the planetarium, all right? I'll be waiting."

I went with him to the door, leaving Joel sitting on the couch looking bruised and angry. Paavo said in a low voice to me, "Why don't you stay a little while? He's not a happy kid, and he took a big chance today. He might have banged his hand really bad. A little company wouldn't hurt him."

"He's a selfish, self-centered pig," I said, not bothering to keep my voice down.

Paavo shook his head. "He doesn't know what you know. Tell him. See if it makes a difference. And Val, be careful going home. Go before dark, okay?"

"Okay," I said.

He left.

So I went back in and sat down across from Joel and I told him.

When I got finished, he said, "Well, I sure can't tell any of that to my parents. If I hadn't been there this afternoon, I wouldn't believe any of it myself. So that really was magic he was doing in the park today, talking to this— this missing statue with his violin?"

"Yes, asking it where it was, see? And it answered through me. That's why I had to be inside the outline of its shadow, so I could stand for the statue, sort of."

He squinted at me. "Does it make sense to you?"

"Does what make sense?"

"The whole thing—the kraken, the magic, the missing statue, those bastards, what do you call them, the Princes?"

"I guess. I haven't thought about it a lot."

"You just believe what he tells you."

"Don't you?"

He flung himself back in the couch and sighed. "All right, all right. He's pretty impressive. More impressive than you even know, if you count the music itself. With those big mitts of his, he shouldn't even be able to *play* the violin. I've never heard a touch like that, a tone. Never. Jesus. My father would flip."

"Sure," I said. "And pay anything. Boy, were you gross there. I was really embarrassed, Joel."

He put his hands behind his head. "You don't know the half of it," he said. "I'm not just trying to cash in on this incredible thing that you've fallen into, you know. It's not as simple as that."

"Tell me how simple it is, then," I said, "but make it fast. I'm supposed to get home before dark, Paavo said."

"Damn straight," he said. "You're the one that's important to him, isn't that obvious? He didn't do any magic with me. He just used me like a goddamn tailor's dummy or something. It's different for you. You're *in* it, you're special."

"I don't feel special," I said.

"You are. I'm—" He jumped up and started pacing. "Accidental, you know? Marginal. Something like that. In everything, not just this. You know that band I'm in, playing guitar? They took me on because their lead man had to go to the West Coast with his parents, and I'd picked up enough to fill in on the electric guitar."

"They wouldn't keep you if you weren't good enough for them," I said, "would they?"

"Nope. But good enough for them isn't particularly good, and besides that—it makes me hungry, playing that music. It makes me feel itchy and hungry, you know? I have to tank up on something to do it for very long at a time."

"Drugs?"

He shrugged. "Nothing hard, don't worry, you're not in the clutches of a dope fiend. Grass, mostly."

"That's probably what makes you hungry," I said, "not one kind of music instead of another."

"Oh, what the hell do you know about it?" he snarled.

I grabbed my school stuff. "I better go home."

"Wait a minute, wait! Don't fly off the handle. God, are you touchy! Listen, I'm not trying to get you to feel sorry for me or anything. I mean, look how I live, it's not so bad, right? But I'd like you to understand how it is."

"Great," I said. "How is it?"

Joel threw himself down on the couch again. "How it is, is lousy."

"Classical music," I said, remembering how he'd looked listening to Paavo play. "The violin. You really love that."

He started pushing a glass ashtray around on the top of the coffee table. "It's in the family, I guess."

"Well, who's stopping you? This city must be full of the best teachers, and your parents are connected."

"That's right. Listen, I started. I played when I was little because everybody around me played or sang or something. I have an older sister, did I tell you? She's married, she teaches piano in one of the best music departments in the country. 'I mean, she's not great, but she's damn good. I used to do some playing with her, duets and things. I studied with good people. I was coming along, not a genius or anything like that, but good, maybe better than good later on.

"So here comes my baby brother and without any instrument at all he takes over. I mean, he just *takes over*. He used to potter around at that piano when he was four, five. We thought he'd be a composer, maybe, if not a pianist. Well, came the day he picked up a bow and started conducting some chamber music they were playing here, my father and some friends. Turned out we had a goddamn prodigy on our hands. His instrument is the orchestra—*all* the instruments, *every* one. He plays the players, or whatever it is that conductors do. It's a mystery to me, believe me."

"So you quit?" I said. "You could play like that, like Paavo, and you just quit?"

"Not like him, that's what I'm saying! And no, I didn't just quit. I lost interest, I practiced less and less. One day I stopped. By then I was fooling around with the electric guitar—I had to do something. They all think I rebelled against the classical mania here and that I was doing my music someplace else, a different way."

He stopped and looked down at his left hand, which he was rubbing again. "Well, actually my mother took it hard. She doesn't like popular music much, especially the heavy amp stuff. She'd feel better, I think, if she knew it was like doodling to me, just fooling around to pass the time. But I can't talk to her about it. I can't talk to any of them."

I said, "I like a lot of popular stuff, myself."

"Me, too," he said. "But it's not the same."

I had sometimes missed not having brothers or sisters of my own, and I sometimes thought I wouldn't mind having a more glamorous parent or two. This tale of Joel's was kind of sobering.

To tell the truth, though, I thought he was more silly than tragic. I mean, in his place I'd saw away on my fiddle with whatever scrap of talent I had and be happy as a clam, tucked warm and cozy in the bosom of my nice, intact, cultured, very comfortable family. Also it struck me as just a tiny bit selfish to be more hung up on this sad story of being only talented, not a genius, than on the possible eating of the whole entire world by the kraken.

On the other hand, it could not be denied that Joel was a good-looking boy, and good-looking people are inclined to get stuck on themselves at one time or another, if not permanently. And I had to admit that he could probably wow the blazes out of everybody on a concert stage with a violin tucked under his chin.

It struck me, too, that for me to be jealous of his bond with Paavo through music (if there was one) in the face of the problem we all had on our hands, well, that was petty, too.

"Hey," I said. "Thanks for telling me. I think I have a better handle on things now. From your point of view, I mean."

"I guess it sounds pretty narrow and egotistical," he said. Which it did, so I said, "Well, a little."

He waved at the pictures on the wall.

"Listen, everybody in this house is some kind of performer, and if you don't think that's a crash course in ego, let me tell you—"

I said, "Sure you can tell me, but not now. It's getting late, and I still have to get back across the park."

"You want me to come with you, in case of the Princes?"

"No, that's okay. Paavo said I can get home okay in daylight."

"Paavo said the Princes were too busy to come bother us this afternoon in the park," he pointed out.

"He's being more careful now. Anyway, Joel, you did enough. I didn't realize, about your hands, you know, not wanting to take any risks with them, being a musician yourself. You better soak the hurt one in hot water for a while. And maybe you could get cleaned up before your parents get home so you don't scare them to death when they see you."

"I guess," he said, walking me to the door. "Thanks for listening. It's not stuff I can talk about with my family. They'd think I was accusing them of pressuring me, which they say they never did. They didn't, either, not con-sciously, anyway. And to my musician-friends, it's all old hat, they don't want to hear it. It's kind of nice to talk to somebody outside of all that."

Somebody totally without talents, I guess he meant. I said, "I may be a writer, myself."

"No kidding," he said. "Stories, or what? My sister thought she was going to be a writer for a while, but she gave it up for the piano."

I wasn't about to admit any more about my writing to somebody I barely knew. "Listen, I've got to go. I'll be waiting for you tomorrow, okay? In the planetarium park."

"You're pretty gutsy, for a girl," he said.

7
Mom's Spy

"**T**ina, where have you been?" my mother said.

Bad luck. She'd come home early, and I was walking in pretty late, to tell the truth. And, it turned out, she had spoken to the doorman downstairs and found out I'd come in late the day before, too.

And she'd noticed that my big framed map of the world was gone from my bedroom wall, along with some stuffed animals left over from when I was a lot younger. I'd been meaning to clear them out anyhow, the animals I mean, so I didn't mind. But Mom was nervous. Maybe she thought I was selling my own stuff to finance some godawful habit.

I have to say I envied Joel being able to lie so casually, even if only to the doorman in his building, saying I was from his school. Well, implying it, anyway. Myself, I am a lousy liar because I tend to forget what I've said by the time I have to repeat the lie or go on from there.

So I don't do it much. It seemed to me that this was one of those necessary times, though. I mean, my mother has told me often enough not to talk to strange men; all mothers say that, and they've got good reasons, too, as anybody knows who reads the papers. She would not be delighted to hear about Paavo.

I said, "I was out with Megan."

Mistake.

Mom had called Megan's mother. She had called Barbara's mother. She had even called Margie Acton's mother, and that was really pushing things.

She sat on the sofa in the living room, my neat, intense mother with the beautiful mascara and the carefully polished nails, and she fixed me with a steely gaze that would have terrified the men she went out with if they'd ever seen it.

"Tina," she said, "you'd better tell me what's going on. I'm on my own with you, but that doesn't mean I don't keep an eye open for your welfare like other parents. It means I have to do it for two, you understand? And I take that responsibility very seriously." I thought for a minute I was in for the lecture about how she was not happy about being a working mother and not having as much time for me as she'd like but she'd get that fixed as soon as she could, if only a decent man would come into her life. I believe there was a time when divorced and working mothers didn't lay things out exactly that clearly to their kids, and frankly I'd just as soon have gone that route, but I guess you get what you get.

This was not, however, that lecture.

"You weren't with Megan or Barbara or Margie," she said. "Is it possible that you were with Joel?"

Wowf. I tried to keep my face still but my mom is nobody's fool, let me tell you, no matter how silly she sounds simpering at some guy on the telephone. I could see she'd spotted something in my expression.

"Joel who?" I said, stalling.

"Joel Wechsler, of course." Mom sat back and watched me. She fiddled with the string of baroque pearls she was wearing. They looked like plastic to me, and I'd said so once and we'd had some words about tact. I did not like her right now because I knew there was no way to turn off her concern, which I really appreciated when I needed it. This was not one of those times. This was a time when she could use that concern to spoil something that belonged to me, myself, alone.

How in the heck did she know about Joel?

She read my mind. "You were seen today," she said. "Going up to Joel's parents' apartment."

God. Was my mother spying on me? Could one of her ex-boyfriends live in Joel's building or something? Would one of them use me as an excuse to call her?

"Well, somebody's wrong, then," I said, but I knew it was all doomed, the whole business.

"I don't think so," my mother said. "Do you remember coming to my office that day I forgot a manuscript, and I asked you to bring it down after school? Do you remember the writer I was having a conference with, the one with the blue hair?"

Did I ever. One of my mother's authors. Oh God. I shrugged.

"Mrs. Teitelbaum," said my mother, "author of *Cat Fancies, The Haunting of Desire,* and *Children of Neglect.* That author. She knows every bargain in New York City, does Mrs. Teitelbaum, and she gets her hair cut by a very,

very chic hairdresser at his own apartment for half the price he charges at the salon. Guess where he lives?"

"She remembered me?" I blurted, giving it all away, but what the heck, my mom is a real terrier about something once she gets her teeth into it. There was no way out of this but right through it. I just hoped it would be quick and relatively painless because I really like my mom, and I wanted to get back to where we could giggle together over Mrs. Teitelbaum's blue hair and her pretty blue fictional imagination, instead of doing this interrogation of yours truly myself over what Mrs. Teitelbaum had said she'd seen.

"Children of Neglect," my mother mused. "You never read that one, did you? Mrs. Teitelbaum's one excursion into serious nonfiction. She loves kids. She never forgets a kid's face. She didn't phone me to report on you, by the way, but to ask a question about her royalty statement. Then she said something about this small world in which I too know the Wechslers, and was I aware that Carlotta Wechsler just loved *Cat Fancies*? I said, 'What Wechslers?' and she told me."

She was smiling. I smiled back.

"Um, well, Mom, I met this boy," I said, and stopped, not knowing where to go from there.

My mom got this revolting, gooey look. "Oh, Tina, of course you did. You had to meet one someday, didn't you? I just wish you hadn't kept it a secret from me. Do you know how that makes me feel?"

We had a very long, heart-to-heart talk which I refuse to go into any more than is absolutely necessary. It was extremely embarrassing. First of all, even though it had been blood-curdlingly clear to both me and Lennie from pretty soon after we noticed each other that we were not destined to spend our lives together, we had done some kissing and exploring around together before giving up out of sheer embarrassment over the determination of Fate to mess us over whenever we were together. It wasn't as if I was completely ignorant, aside from the explanations Mom had given me when I got my first period.

Secondly, I didn't have the feelings about Joel that my mother insisted on assuming I had, but here came all this carefully nondirective advice meant to keep me from getting in over my head with somebody I didn't even like much. I just had to sit there squirming and take it as if it applied.

She told me what Mrs. Teitelbaum had passed on to her: that Joel was a sweet boy although inclined to be moody and rather self-absorbed, and that he had stopped going to a special school for artistic kids when he'd quit studying the violin, to the shock of his parents, who continued to hope that he would return one day to the fold; and that it had worried Mrs. Teitelbaum that the poor boy had been robbed in the park, or so the doorman had told her, and was I all right or had I been involved too— along with the elderly gentleman who had accompanied us upstairs, some musical friend of the family's, no doubt?

Agent Teitelbaum had spotted Paavo too, of course.

"Yes," I said. "He's a retired musician who plays chamber music with Joel's dad sometimes. Joel's parents were both busy, so Joel went to him first about the mugging. It wasn't serious, nobody got hurt."

We didn't stay with Paavo or the mugging for long, though. The important part of this conversation was the lecture on men, which was what Mom concentrated on.

I'd had this lecture before, and sitting through it again didn't help my patience. I was feeling very jittery, wondering if Mom would end up doing something really weird and impossible, like trying to forbid me to see Joel again. You never knew with her. It could depend on how things were going between her and Mr. Editor.

But she ended with, "I hope Joel treats you well, Tina, and I hope you maintain the standards of someone who respects herself and other people," and so on. The usual. I'd been hearing it for a long time.

I'd have liked to tell her that she had nothing to worry about, that Joel and I didn't really hit it off too well, but there was no way to do that.

Then she said, "Tomorrow, Tina, I'd like you home right away after school to do something special for me. I'd like you to stay here and see if the landlord sends anyone up here to rip off anything more of ours, all right?"

She meant that I'd seen enough of Joel for a while and so I'd better get otherwise occupied. That's how she was, blowing hot one minute and cold the next. It was really impossible.

"Alone, Tina," she said. "All right?"

"What are you going to do, get the doorman to spy on me while I'm supposed to be spying on the landlord?" I said.

So we had a fight after all, and the result was that I was told I absolutely had to come straight home from school the next day, or else. Or else what exactly was not spelled out. My mother preferred to work on the theory, I think, that a vague sort of threat was more effective than something specific that I could think about and weigh in the balance, so to speak.

What she would have said about the Princes and Paavo I did not know, but I have to admit it crossed my mind to come out with all of it. I mean, she and I had lived together a long time, on our own and backing each other up a lot in spite of certain differences. As I said, she was no fool. I was curious about what she would make of Paavo.

She'd probably think he was an old mole-ster, that's what. I kept my mouth shut. I felt mean and angry about the whole thing.

Nobody was going to keep me out of the most important business in my life.

I set my alarm and put it under my pillow, and it woke me at one A.M. I sneaked into the kitchen, shut the door, and phoned Joel in the dark, looking out the window into the air shaft where I used to hear Mr. Vishinsky's music.

I'd gotten the number from the phone in Joel's living room, just in case, and I hoped that his family stayed up late, which I thought was pretty likely. My mom went out with a play director for a while, and he said all performers have weird hours because of doing their work in the evening and having to wind down afterwards. It's funny, the useless pieces of information you can remember when they suddenly get useful.

I had kind of liked the director, too, and the idea of the glamorous theater. But Mom had ditched him, or he had ditched her, so that was that.

A woman with a hoarse voice answered the phone, Mrs. Rouse, probably.

"I'm sorry," I said, "but I really need to talk to Joel. He's been tutoring me in math for a test, and I think I left some notes with him. I need him to bring them to school tomorrow. Could you wake him for me? It's important."

One way or another, he got on the line. "Tina? What are you doing calling up so late?"

I told him about my mom putting her oar in. One thing about Joel, he knew how to keep his mouth shut until you got finished.

"Shit," he muttered when I was all through.

"Listen, it doesn't have to make problems if we don't let it," I said, hoping I was right. "Here's the thing, though: my doorman has to see me here tomorrow right after school, no taking time out at the planetarium park. Can you bring Paavo over here? No, not here exactly— upstairs, onto the roof. I'll open our windows. Ask him to play a little music into the air shaft. I'll hear and I'll come up and join you."

"What if he can't do magic on your roof?" he said.

"Just bring him, Joel. I have to be here, and he needs me to do Jagiello's voice." I was scared to death that Joel would find some way to finish the magic questioning of Jagiello without me.

"Won't your doorman tell your mom we came?"

"You don't come through my lobby," I said, and I explained to him how our building had a service door, adjoining the big co-op next to us that had been a hotel before. Our building had been their annex or something, and if you knew where to find it, there was a door connecting the basements. All he had to do was get into Fudge Tower—that was what the kids in my building called the co-op because it was fudge-colored—take the elevator down into the basement, and come up from the laundry room in our basement on the service elevator, which didn't get much use because, as my mother said, we didn't get much service.

Joel was really intrigued by all of this. I gave him the name of a dentist who had an office in the Fudge so he could tell the Fudge doorman that he and Paavo were going there.

"Smart," Joel said. "Do people get caught doing this?"

8

Rooftop Magic

They didn't get caught.

Which is how, the next afternoon, I was standing in the shadow of the elevator housing on our roof, waiting to hear Paavo's music-questions and to bring him Jagiello's answers.

"This is good," he'd said, when I came up to meet them both. It was bright and sunny and so spacious up there. I had almost forgotten how terrific our roof was, with a great view of the waves of other rooftops receding all around, and the Hudson River, and the dark outline of the Palisades to the west. I went up on the roof a lot when I was a kid, but then some people moved in who walked their dogs there and everybody got in the habit of not going up there anymore, for obvious reasons.

The dog-people eventually moved out. Now mostly we got grown-ups sunbathing with their radios on as if they were at the beach, at least if the weather was good. The kids in the building only went up if they thought they might catch a glimpse of something interesting; you know.

There were no sunbathers that afternoon. It was pretty chilly. Paavo should have been cold in his light jacket, but I guess he wasn't because he hadn't even bothered to button the collar of his shirt. He got Joel to stand on the elevator housing and drew on the roof surface the same way he'd drawn on the paving at the park. I stood in the outline and waited.

Paavo said, "In a new place like this, I better call Jagiello first and get his attention turned this way. He was talking Shakespeare, you said?"

He shut his eyes a minute, and then he recited, "Virtue he had, deserving to command; his brandished sword did blind men with his beams; his arms spread wider than a dragon's wings."

That sounded like our old Jagiello, all right. Then Paavo began to play on the violin that Joel had brought.

But this violin wouldn't sing to me, not in words. What happened was not the dark voice at all, but a huge rush of grinding, roaring noise and shaking, as if the ground was rippling underfoot. Suddenly there was this sharp pain over my eye and next thing I knew I was lying on my back, staring at a lot of sky.

Paavo hunkered down next to me and put his hand on my head and looked hard into my face with those odd-shaped gray eyes.

"Hey," I said. "I just remembered something." I sat up, feeling dizzy but okay. "The explosion in the subway! That was just like the explosion in the subway."

"In the subway?" Paavo said. "What explosion?"

We walked along beside the parapet of the roof and I told them about it.

Paavo laughed. "Sure, the subway! What did Jagiello tell us? Darkness, quiet, and then noise, voices like from a crowd, vibration? There was no explosion. That was just the air being displaced when the statue was suddenly popped down there, boom. Well." He stopped and braced his hands wide apart on the parapet and frowned down at the street way below. "We got real trouble now. The subway is the kraken's territory. It's hiding out down there while it gathers its strength to break out onto the surface here. You know that day I was on the train with you, Val? I was taking soundings to see how strong the kraken's hold was down there."

"We still don't know where Jagiello is, though," Joel said. "The subway's a huge system."

"We could start at the Eighty-first Street station," I said.

"Start what, though?" Joel said. "And if we find it, how can we get it out? We're talking about a bronze statue, you know? A couple of tons of metal."

Paavo put away the violin, which he handled as tenderly as he'd handled his own, I noticed. "That's a nice fiddle," he said. "With my own instrument, I could bring out something that was lost to me. But to bring this bronze horse-and-rider out of the kraken's grip and back to its post in the park, now—I don't know. Must be something we can do, though. Depends."

I was watching him, and I saw how his face got grave, and his eyes had a look as if he could see way past the Palisades and all of New Jersey and the farthest edge of the world. A cold feeling came into my chest, and I deliberately looked away because I was scared.

The rooftop seemed suddenly very exposed and scary, and I had a wild fear that somebody—the Princes, or some friend of my mother's—might be watching from a neighboring rooftop. But it was so chilly that nobody else was out, not even on the terraces where sometimes you see people watering their potted plants. You forget how cold it can be on the top of a sixteen-story building, without the deep canyons of the streets to cut the wind.

We huddled in the shelter of the elevator housing and went over our escape plans again. The idea was for Paavo and Joel to get out the way they'd come in, without my doorman seeing them, as if they'd finished their dental appointment in the Fudge. I would slip out a little later and meet them at the Eighty-first Street station on Central Park West, where the explosion had happened.

At the Eighty-first Street station, Joel paid for our tokens. We wandered along the uptown platform wondering what we were looking for.

The only odd thing I noticed right away was a faint, funny smell in the air from the dark subway tunnel. Paavo noticed, too. He wrinkled his nose. He walked along, carrying the violin case and looking carefully at the tracks and the grates in the ceiling over the tracks, and the graffiti on the ads along the tiled walls.

We headed down the stairs to the level of the uptown tracks. A train came in, a few people got out, a man sleeping on a bench turned over and slept some more, and the train pulled out. Joel kicked at the wall, staring impatiently around.

I turned and I saw the blue metal wall at the end of the platform, and my heart gave this boom in my ribs.

See, most platforms end with a plain tiled wall like all the rest of the subway walls. The only place I knew of with an L-shaped blue metal wall, a partition that closed off one whole end of the platform into some kind of storage room, I guess, was up in the Ninety-sixth Street station on Central Park West. I knew because I used to get off there to visit Granny Gran, when she was still living in her own apartment on Ninety-fifth.

The blue wall was made of painted steel with sort of raised stripes up and down it and had a blue steel door set in it with a knob and a plain flat lock, and what was it doing here at Eighty-first Street?

Joel said, "They must have put one up here too, and you just never noticed. Or else it's new."

"No," I said. "It's the same one. It's got the same stuff scratched into the paint." Kids had put their names on it, of course.

"Don't touch it," Paavo said. "Go upstairs, ask questions."

Joel and I went. The lady in the change booth looked bored. No, she said, that wall had always been there. Was there one up at Ninety-sixth too? Sure. What was it for? Equipment, she said, and would we please get out of the way so people could buy their tokens?

What equipment? She didn't know.

Who had the key? She didn't know and if we didn't get going she was going to call a transit cop.

"Okay," Paavo said, when we reported back to him. "We wait."

We waited for the next train to come and take away the six people on the platform. Noboby else came down. Paavo took his bow out of the violin case. He stepped up to the steel wall and rapped on it with the bow tip.

From inside came a loud clanging in answer.

In the tunnel behind us, where the next train should come from, I heard a kind of whispering, grumbling, shifting, shuffling noise, far off but getting closer. With it came a stronger smell, a nasty sour bite in the air.

"What's going on?" Joel said nervously.

Paavo took hold of the metal handle of the door and pulled.

The door didn't budge, but there came another tremendous, shivering clang from behind it, and the noises in the tunnel got louder and thicker with a high, edgy tone threading through them like a question asked in a scream. I was about to scream myself.

"Go!" Paavo said, grabbing up the violin case, and we tore out of there and into the open air. "Don't stop here," he panted, "keep going!"

We dodged across Central Park West against the light and flopped down on a bench next to the park wall.

For a few minutes nobody said anything. Paavo put his bow back in Joel's case. Then he said, "Anyplace around here for a cup of coffee?"

The three of us ended up at a corner table in Lox Populi, where Paavo demolished two cream pastries and all the pickles in the little tub on the table. He must have had a metabolism wilder than mine, because even the way he ate, he wasn't at all fat, just solid and sinewy. He sat hunched over the table with his hands wrapped around his coffee mug and he said, "Well, you got a good sniff of the kraken down there. Not so nice, eh?"

"Was that what it was?" Joel shifted around uncomfortably, looking over his shoulder at the door. "It stunk. Well, what are we going to do?"

"We know where Jagiello is," Paavo said.

"That was him?" Joel said. "Making all that clanging noise?"

"That was him, but he's stuck in there," Paavo said.

"Now that you know exactly where he is, can you play him out?" I said.

"Not without my own fiddle," Paavo said. "And I don't have time to build up another one. So that's out."

"Can we get some help?" I said. I didn't want to mention Sorcery Hall again in front of Joel. He was already horning in on my business more than I liked, though I was glad he'd been around when the Princes showed up.

Paavo said, "I don't think so. It's up to us to get that damn blue door open for Jagiello."

It was funny hearing him swear just like any regular person, only more delicate, somehow. A lot of grown-ups have really foul mouths these days, even about little things.

"How do we do that?" Joel said. "The kraken was coming for us, right? It knew we were there?"

"Yah," Paavo said. He stretched. "Okay, look. I got to go get some rest. We're running out of time, though, and now that you've got the kraken's scent and it's got yours— well, be careful, you two. Tomorrow you come find me at

Grant's Tomb, all right? I want to do some patching there. The Princes wrote some bad words on it. They got it almost down to no power, and one way or another we're going to need all the power we can get hold of."

"Where are you going now?" I said.

"Downtown. They got some places you can sleep."

Joel got red in the face. "You mean those flophouses for bums? That's not—you don't belong—I think you should come home with me. My folks would be pleased to put you up. I'll explain—"

"Explain what?" said Paavo, rubbing at the side of his neck and looking at Joel patiently. He rubbed that same place often, and I'd noticed a sort of darkish mark like a bruise there.

"Well, I don't have to say anything about the kraken or any of that," Joel said. "See, my dad takes in—extends his hospitality to all kinds of musical people. He'd be honored to have you stay over, honest."

Paavo thought about it, looking unfocused and tired. He shook his head. "Thanks, but I better not. Things could get to be a problem."

He downed the last of his coffee and dug around in his pockets, and then he turned to me and he said, "Val, you got something for a tip?"

Without a word Joel and I emptied our pockets and shoved this pathetic pile of change over to him.

"Thanks," he said. He took the money, left a tip, and stood up. "Tomorrow," he said. "After school. Grant's Tomb."

I said, "What if something comes up in the meantime? How can we find you?"

"You know how to get in touch," he said. "It's a little clumsy, but it's the best we can do."

He left.

"He should have come home with me," Joel muttered.

"Don't you know anything?" I said. "He's worried that the kraken or the Princes might get after him, and he didn't want to take a chance on your parents getting caught in the middle. Or you."

"I can take care of myself," he said. "I did okay with the Princes, didn't I? You'd have been in real hot water if I hadn't been along."

"Listen, Joel," I said, "let's just remember whose business this all is, all right? Paavo is here because *I* got in touch, because of what *my* grandmother told me."

"Oh boy," he said, "we're trying to save the world here, and you're getting possessive."

"You're the one who's acting possessive," I said.

Joel stared at the door after Paavo. "God, if only I could get him to play for my father!"

I walked out and went home.

9
Grounded

There was lots and lots of homework to do. I hadn't exactly been keeping up with my assignments. The weekend was only one day away, finally, so I hoped I'd have time to get to everything then.

If there was a weekend. If the kraken didn't gobble everything up first.

Mom called from her office downtown, checking up on me: where had I been, when she'd expressly told me to come home and stay there? Fight, yell, hang up, trouble later, but she didn't know anything new. There was no way she could find out I'd been with Joel and Paavo unless her spy network caught me again. I figured the odds on that one were in my favor for a change.

I sat home and read the paper (we got our deliveries again after that disastrous *Times*less Sunday). It had stories about a subway train that had derailed itself somehow and injured a lot of passengers, and about the collapse of a new section of the West Side Highway. Could these things be due to the kraken flexing its muscles? I sat and shivered with the paper jiggling in my hands, because I knew they were. The kraken was getting ready to come out. In the meantime it was making these forays in the subway and the sewer passages and the conduits for power and water and all that stuff.

This was my first experience with a secret so huge and incredible that it was hardly a secret at all. I mean, you could scream it from the housetops and it wouldn't make any difference because nobody would believe you. They'd only lock you up for observation.

I couldn't watch TV. I couldn't read. Finally, I called up Granny Gran in New Jersey.

She recognized my voice—that was a good start— and started complaining to me about the new person next door to her who played the radio too loud.

"Granny Gran," I said, "somebody's here from Sorcery Hall. He says we've got real trouble. He says there's a kraken."

She said, "What did you say, Vee?" She always called me that, Vee for Valentine. "I don't understand you."

Well, it went on like that for a while. "Is this one of those books you read all the time, about talking unicorns and so on? Are you telling me a story? You're not getting all involved in those Dungeons and Dragons games, are you?" She sounded very compos mentis, but just out of it.

I had this sinking feeling that Paavo was right about not bothering her, that it had been a mistake. Before I talked to her I could always tell myself that she might be able to help. But now I couldn't kid myself about that anymore. She didn't have a clue, and that was that.

"When are you coming to visit me, Vee?" she said.

"Soon as I can, Gran," I said, feeling very depressed.

"You could take the subway," she said.

I sat up straight. You couldn't, actually, take the subway out there or anywhere near there. "Gran," I said, "what about the subway?"

"Even underground," she said, "the way you open a door is with a key."

"What?" I said.

"A key," she said. "You use a key. Good night now, lovie, come and see me soon."

And she hung up, bam.

I sat there on the bed itching to call her back. But this was the thing about Granny Gran: when she said goodbye and hung up, bam like that, that was it. It always meant she was unplugging the phone and wouldn't be answering for a while because she had other things to do.

A key? You open a door with a key? Even in the subway. Well, we'd asked about the key to the blue door. No dice. The token lady didn't even know who might have a key, or if she did know she wouldn't say.

I lay back on my bed, thinking about the blue door and the scars in the paint and the brass plate over the keyhole, and how the wall clanged after Paavo tapped it with his bow . . .

Then I figured that since Mom was after me anyway about having gone out today when she'd told me not to, I might as well finish the job. I went downstairs and walked out of my lobby past the afternoon doorman—who'd already done his informing for the day—and up to the Ninety-sixth Street and Central Park West subway station.

The original blue wall was there, with the identical names scratched into the blue paint, the identical scratches on the lock plate, and the identical answers from the guy in the token booth: no, he didn't have a key, and he didn't know who did or what they kept in there except that it was some kind of maintenance equipment, and no, he didn't know anything about another place just like it down at the Eighty-first Street station.

I went home and started making spaghetti for dinner.

Mom came in singing. She had a date with Mr. Editor, thank goodness. We fenced around about my having gone out in defiance of her orders, but she was so pleased about her date and about nothing more being missing, in spite of my desertion of my post, that it was all okay.

Next morning I found my bookshelves completely empty. My whole collection was gone, including a hardcover copy of *The Secret Garden* from the secondhand bookstore on Fourteenth Street and a book of old maps from Uncle Tim. (Our Manhattan telephone directories were gone too.)

I was furious. There was nothing I could do. I shut my door and didn't say anything to Mom. She would just tell me that Sam or some nameless thug hired by the landlord had sneaked in during the night and stolen my books while I slept, and frankly, there was no alternative explanation I could offer. Not without blowing everything completely.

That day in French class I sort of woke up. That is, I was cringing in my seat, listening to Froggy Fergusson reading with his awful, awful accent, when all of a sudden I heard the booming sound that the hall doors make in that particular hallway if you push through them fast, and I remembered: the explosion, the hard thing whacking me over my eye—

At lunch period I called Joel's school with an emergency message for him. Using my mom's telephone voice, which I had recently perfected, I told them I was his new shrink. They got him on the phone.

I told him to meet me at the Eighty-first Street station right away and then I hung up, bam, like Granny Gran.

He met me, which means he climbed out of a taxi lugging the loaner-violin case and looking furious. He showed the cab driver some money and told him to wait.

"What is this?" he said to me. "What do you think you're doing?"

"When the subway exploded, or whatever happened, something flew out and smacked me over the eyebrow, right here."

"Where that mark is?" he said.

"What mark?" I said, a little shaken up by this. I hadn't noticed any mark.

"Well, you have a red spot there."

"Listen, Joel," I said, "I know what happened. The key, the key to that lock on the blue door downstairs in this station is what came flying out of there. It hit me, it bounced right off me and landed someplace around here. Help me look for it."

"Now?" he said.

"Of course now! Have you been watching the papers? I don't think we have a lot of time. Some creepy things have been happening, and it's getting worse."

"The awning was missing from the front of my building this morning," he said. "Because you were there, right? You're what they call a vector, at least for some of these weird things that are going on."

"Joel, I am not carrying a disease!"

"Not exactly, but you are a little dangerous to be around, aren't you?" God, was he going to walk away from all this because the kraken, looking for the key, kept making these blind grabs in my direction? Could I blame him if he did?

He scratched his neck under the scarf he wore. "Do you remember a key, an actual key?"

"No," I said, very relieved that he was sticking around. "But I remember what it felt like when it hit me, and it could have been a key. It was small and cold. And I think it marked me like this to show, to—to claim me. That's why I've been involved from the beginning: because the key happened to hit me." And the key hit me, I didn't tell Joel, because of my connection to Sorcery Hall through my Granny Gran.

"That was days ago," Joel said. "You won't find it. If it's been lying on the sidewalk all this time, it could have been kicked anyplace by now, or picked up by anyone."

"No," I said, though so far I hadn't had any luck and I was pretty worried. "It's waiting for us to find it."

"What about the Princes?" he said, glancing around. "Any sign of them?"

I lost my patience. "Look, if you're scared, go back to school. If not, help me look. I want to bring the key to Paavo today."

Joel paid the cab driver, and we looked. There wasn't anything: just squares of concrete, and the curb and the gutter, and the metal skirting around the subway entrance. We wandered around glaring at the ground. Somehow a lot of time went by, and pretty soon, Joel reminded me, we should be heading uptown to meet Paavo at Grant's Tomb.

I didn't want to go empty-handed, not when I knew what I was looking for and where to look for it.

"Maybe Paavo has some way of locating it right away," Joel said, "or maybe he could pick up the trail of whoever's got it."

"Nobody's got it," I growled. My eyes were tearing with frustration. "It's got to be here! It hit me and bounced off—"

I stood there thinking. I thought about how when Barbara first started wearing contact lenses, the hard kind, the left one used to pop out a lot because she blinked too hard when it was bothering her. We did a lot of patting the ground in some pretty strange places. You haven't been in the pits until you've groped the floor of a movie theater in the dark among the gum wads and sticky soda spills, looking for a lost lens.

We both got very good at hearing where the lens landed. That tiny click is all you need to get a good idea, more or less, of where to start patting.

So when the key had hit my forehead, where had it landed afterward?

I turned around and stood as close to where I'd been standing that day as I could remember.

"What are you doing?" Joel said. "You look weird."

I told him to shush.

I had been standing here, by the subway entrance, fishing around in my bookbag for my math assignment, and muttering. The ground shook, and something tapped me hard over the eye, and then—

"There was no sound," I said. "It didn't make any sound!"

"You mean it disappeared, like all those other things?" Joel said. "Come on, Tina—"

"No, no," I said, "that happens with a contact lens, too. If there's no sound, you know it never reached the floor. It's hung up somewhere on your clothes, or it landed in the book you were reading, something like that."

"What were you wearing?"

"I don't know, exactly, but if I look in my closet, I'll remember. The key must be caught in a pocket or a cuff!"

"Where're you going?" he said.

"Home! To look through my clothes!"

At the door to my building, I told him to wait downstairs for me. I wasn't about to have Joel come look over everything I owned.

I went ripping through my closet, my dresser, my laundry hamper, looking for what I'd been wearing that day—the cuffless jeans with pockets too tight to jam anything into, let alone for something to fall in, the boots, the yellow shirt, my fuzzy jacket.

There was nothing in any of them, not even in the pockets of the fuzzy jacket.

I stood there feeling sick with failure. What was I going to tell Paavo?

Then Mom came in. "Tina? Are you home?" I could tell by her voice that something was wrong and going to get wronger.

"I forgot my English paper and Mr. Chernick told me to go home and get it. I'm just leaving."

"Is that so?" she said. She was in the living room, looking through the mail, I think. "I had a call from school a little while ago. I hear that you not only flunked a math test, you're behind with two book reports and three weeks late with a presentation for social studies class. On top of which, they told me you'd vanished from school today."

There wasn't a lot to say to this, so I didn't say anything. I looked out my bedroom window. Joel was hanging around across the street. I made go-away signs. He didn't see or didn't mean to go away, because he didn't budge. Well, if Mom hadn't spotted him on her way in, maybe we were okay.

She came and stood in the doorway to my room, probably expecting to find Joel in there with me. Even though I was alone as requested, I saw her get that bland, above-it-all look that meant real trouble. "And here you've been neatening up your room. What a beautiful job. I'm really impressed."

The room did look as if it had been burgled by a troop of rhinoceroses. "I'm looking for something," I said.

"Oh?" she said. "What? China?" She waited for me to admire that and then she really let loose: "I'm looking for something, too. I'm looking for my kitchen linoleum, and I'm looking for some galley proofs that have gone walkabout all on their own, and I'm looking for the phone call I should have had by now from my nice but very, very busy lawyer. Most of all, I'm looking for a little quiet in that madhouse I call my office, not nagging phone calls from school telling me that my daughter is turning into a cretinous delinquent. I'm looking for a house I can step into without wondering how I got into a pigpen by mistake. You know Mrs. Sanchez comes tomorrow. You know she isn't going to clean up any of this incredible decor you've designed for yourself—"

"I wasn't going to ask her—"

"What will happen will be a phone call to me from Mrs. Sanchez, complaining about the state of your room and how she can't clean in here when it's like this. She'll take up my time with a detailed list of grievances going back three and a half years and wind up by threatening to quit."

"I'll fix it," I mumbled.

It was amazing to me, how my soft, sweet, flirtatious mother, who had often told me to try to soften my own attitude and to hide my brains so as not to scare away the boys that she was also so worried about, had this other side to her that I don't think she realized existed. This was the tough side, the smart, ambitious woman who held down the job that kept us both in spaghetti. What she always said was how she wanted to find some nice guy to look after both of us. What she did was run her life and mine, when I let her, with a hand of steel. Sometimes a very heavy hand of steel. I really hated her at this particular moment, the way you can only hate your mother.

"Yes, you certainly will fix it," she said. "But first you are going to bring your schoolbooks into the kitchen, and you and I are going to sit down and waste more of my time—my most precious time, the kind I use to try to repair myself and stay sane through something I think they call relaxation. We are going to spend some of that time going over your situation in school and setting up a schedule, Tina, according to which you will get everything that's owing done. Late, but done. You understand?"

"I said I'll fix it!" I screamed. "I'll fix it, the room and the work and the whole damn thing if you'll just leave me alone and let me do it my own way!"

"Schoolbooks," she said. "Now, Tina. In the kitchen. This shambles can wait."

"Shambles means slaughterhouse," I said. "I haven't killed anything in here." Yet. "And don't call me Tina, it's babyish and stupid. *I* never asked to be called Tina. I hate my name."

Which was news to me. I didn't know it until I said it.

"Really?" my mother said sweetly. "That was your own name for yourself before you could pronounce Valentine, so don't blame me. I'll be waiting for you in the kitchen."

You can't win.

I needed a piece of paper and something to weight it with so I could drop a note down to Joel from the window. I emptied my bookbag out onto the bed.

But what was I going to write? Sorry, no key, can't come down, grounded by mother for messiness and stupidity which is really just not having enough time to manage Sorcery Hall and the kraken and my schoolwork all at once.

Groping around in the heap of books and papers and notebooks and school junk from my bookbag, I found something small and heavy to wrap my note around.

It was a key.

10

The Abandoned Station

A plain brass-colored key with a jigsaw-jaggedy edge and a flowery design stamped on the round part that you hold. I had no more doubt of what it was than of my own, well, my name.

The thing had bounced off my cretinous, hard little head right into my open bookbag. I was so relieved I almost whooped out loud. I sat down on the bed to write.

First I had to accept the fact that not only were Joel and Paavo going to go on without me, they were probably going to wind up the whole business without me, and there wasn't a thing I could do about it. Not unless I wanted to risk having the world gobbled up, starting with the West Side Highway or what was left of it.

So I wrote a note, gritting my teeth the whole time. I didn't care about Joel, but Paavo wasn't going to think much of me when he found out why I couldn't come down. Grounded, like a ten-year-old!

I know kids who would do whatever they wanted and ignore what their parents said, but I just couldn't do that. Not with my mom on her own the way she was, and the two of us running the household together. I know who gets the blame when a kid living with only her mother looks bad, and besides, I was kind of proud of how well I got along with her, considering. I didn't want to ruin it. We had a deal. She didn't go through my closets and things, and I didn't duck out on her rules, much. Mutual toleration.

I leaned out the window.

There was Joel, standing on the curb now and staring up. There was no way I could miss with that key. I am a champion thrower, thanks to having to throw stones to defend myself from country dogs around my uncle's place in Pennsylvania in the summers. I crumpled the piece of notebook paper around the key and leaned out.

"Tina," he yelled, "what are you doing?"

From behind me I heard my mom coming, yelling, "Tina, what are you doing?"

I dropped the little package. It was lighter than I'd thought and veered on a breeze. Joel, loaded down with his books and the violin case, made a clumsy dive after it. My mother banged the window shut and grabbed my arm in her grip of steel, and the rest of the evening is not worth telling about.

Not that my mom is any kind of child abuser, but when she gets pushed over the edge into one of her strict fits, she becomes a kind of maximum-security warden, with my best interests at heart.

I was still putting my things away at about one A.M., in the dark, just stuffing them any old where. Mom had told me to go to bed, but once I got started cleaning up I wasn't about to stop and leave more to do tomorrow. Tomorrow, which was Saturday at last, I was reserving for hearing from Joel and Paavo all about how they saved the world.

Only it didn't happen that way.

For one thing, I woke up that Saturday morning and found that my bookbag, which I had emptied out onto the bed the day before thank goodness, was gone. The kraken had finally gotten as close as it was going to get to the key.

But if Joel and Paavo had stopped the kraken, wouldn't the vanished things be coming back, not more things disappearing?

And the day looked funny. Although it was spring, the sky was cloudy and cold again, sullen-looking, broody, and mean.

I started to worry, but for the moment there was nothing I could do about it. I settled down to one of my neglected assignments. ("You can wait to see your friend Joel until you've caught up with your schoolwork." "You told me that five times already." "Well, I'm telling you again. How can I explain to you how distressing it is for me, Tina, to find that I can't seem to trust you anymore? You're not to sneak off to meet him, do you understand?" "If I want to meet Joel someplace I'm sure not going to sneak." Etc. Our relationship was definitely on the downslope.)

I could afford to be patient. I knew Mom had a brunch date downtown with one of her authors, which was one reason she'd been able to come home early the day before—because she was set up for work on the weekend. She certainly was not going to take me along, and there was no way to lock me in.

I hung out the window after she left to make sure she really did go. As soon as she'd turned the corner, I zipped downstairs and out through Fudge Tower, and I headed toward the Eighty-first Street station.

Paavo was standing on a corner on Columbus Avenue, drinking Coke from one of those wax cups. Mom had probably walked right past him. He looked gloomy and a little rumpled. He looked old.

"What happened?" I said. I had a horrible feeling the answer was going to be pretty bad.

It was. "Joel tried to use the key. The kraken has him."

I almost sat down on the sidewalk, but managed instead to swivel around and plump myself against the wall next to Paavo. For a minute I couldn't say anything. I was full of this big, blaring feeling of UNFAIR. It wasn't supposed to be like this. You don't get involved in magical adventures to lose. Not in books, anyway.

"I didn't mean to scare you," Paavo said. He put his arm around my shoulders and gave me a quick little hug. "Joel isn't dead. But the kraken is holding him."

"He was supposed to take the key to you at Grant's Tomb!" I could feel my chin start to wobble the way it does before I'm going to cry, and I was desperate not to cry in front of Paavo.

Paavo shook his head. "He came looking, but I was late. I got held up. I don't have all my strength here; this place slows me down. Anyhow, he didn't wait. He went to the station alone and tried to use the key. He's not the right one to do that, so the kraken grabbed him. The only reason it couldn't take the key from him then and there was, he's got my bow in his violin case. The kraken can only move him around, it can't really touch him, so long as he hangs onto that."

"He was supposed to come and get you, the stupid *bastard!*" I yelled. "Who does he think he is, Jagiello on his bronze horse? He was supposed to give the key to *you.*"

"Listen, Valentine," Paavo said, "you got to understand, for a kid like Joel—in this world a boy who studies classical music, right away he's got a strike against him. He's not allowed to fight because he has to take care of his hands, right? He spends a lot of time doing something most kids his age don't understand. So some people tell him he's a sissy, you know? He gets pushy about it, he takes chances to prove he's tough, he's regular."

"But he's not studying," I blubbered. "He told me! He used to, but he quit."

"He's been practicing on the sly," Paavo said. "Even if he really wants to quit, he hasn't been able to."

"How do you know that?" I said.

"He wears a scarf all the time, doesn't he? Pulled up high on the sides of his neck? It's to hide this." He showed me the place on the left side of his own neck, under his jaw, where his creased, leathery skin had that dark mark on it, like a large irritated callus. "The fiddler's brand," he said. "All fiddle players have one, from holding the instrument there. He hides his brand because he's addicted to the fiddle and he's angry and ashamed about it."

"What are we wasting sympathy on him for?" I bawled. "I don't care if he fiddles a hole in his neck from one side to the other. He'd deserve it! If he'd only waited! What are we supposed to do now? If he'd used his brains and been a little more patient, it might all be over by now, and the kraken would be gone!"

Paavo, completely ignoring my gulps and snuffles, said reasonably, "Okay, you're right. The reasons he did what he did don't matter right now. The damage is done. Let's think if we can fix it."

He was so calm and deliberate, I felt worse than before.

"What are we going to do?" I wailed.

"Find him and get the key," Paavo said. "That's what we got to do."

That stopped the tears right there. I said, "Are you certain the kraken's got him? How do you know for sure?" I think what I meant was, How do you know he's really still alive?

"I'll show you. Look." Paavo emptied what was left of his Coke onto the sidewalk and took me over to a fire hydrant that was leaking water from one of its spouts or whatever they are. He rinsed his cup and filled it about halfway with water from the hydrant, and then he whistled a little tune and stirred the water with his finger.

The surface cleared and I could see Joel. It was just like looking at a reflection. He was sitting on the ground in some enclosed place with weird, dim light and a jumbled-up confusion of color behind him—graffiti!

"He's in a subway station," I said. "That's graffiti all over the walls of a station. Why doesn't he just walk out?"

"He can't see," Paavo said very softly. "The kraken has him bound with darkness. He doesn't know where he is, except that he's down in the subway."

"You mean he's blind?" I was really horrified. I mean, Joel was only sixteen!

"That's how it seems to him," Paavo nodded. "He feels bad, you can see that."

I sure could. Joel was sitting all bent over, with his violin case across his knees and his face hidden, and I was just as glad I couldn't see his expression.

"But he'll be all right, I mean he'll be able to see if we get him out of there, right?" I said.

"I think so," Paavo said. "But we got to find him first; him and the key."

"That's easy!" I said. "He's in the old IRT station at Ninety-first and Broadway, the one they closed up ages ago! There's still a way into it from the street, my friend Barbara and I discovered it years ago. That's how come the graffiti writers can get in there and write on the walls. All we have to do is get over there and go down into the station and bring Joel out!"

Paavo looked at me for a minute. "That simple?" he said.

"Well, I don't know," I said, "I've never gone down there in daylight, and also you get pretty dirty."

I was looking at his rust brown suit that was just starting to look a little grubby from being worn every day.

"We'll try," he said.

So we went over to Ninety-first Street and Broadway, and I didn't see any way that Paavo and I were going to be able to sneak down into that station in broad daylight. You can't just walk over to the grating in the sidewalk, yank it up, and skip down the steps into the station without somebody noticing. The time Barbara and I did it, we'd waited until about two in the morning. Even then a couple of people saw us but I guess they didn't say anything.

"It's that grating," I said, pointing. You can see the steps dropping away underneath into the gloom, covered with trash and butts and whatnot that people drop and kick through the grating. The opening is so small and square that I wondered if Paavo could get his shoulders through it. Altogether I was amazed that Barbara and I had actually had the nerve to go down there at all, especially in the middle of the night.

"Okay," Paavo said, "go in when I tell you." He started humming through his nose, this high, soft sound that made my skin prickle, and he turned quickly in a circle all in one place. A little wind came up and began to whip around us, around and around, tighter and tighter and louder and louder. Old papers and fast-food wrappers and butts and rags zipped by us in a tight little whirlwind. I couldn't see through it anymore, and I was getting scared.

Paavo, still humming, leaned down and got hold of the rim of the grate and heaved it up and open: "Go!" he said. I went, bent almost double to get through the opening, into the cold, nasty smell of the place. He didn't follow me. I was supposed to do this alone? Looked like I was. I crouched on the steps, underneath the sidewalk, and I breathed that ugly cold stink and looked into the dimness of the few faint bulbs always left on here, shining coldly off the scribbled walls. I wished I was someplace else.

Above me the wind whined and whined and papers scraped on the concrete. I went down a few more steps and called, "Joel!"

No answer. Far away I heard a train rumbling in the tunnel.

I went down into the eerie stillness of the station. Every square inch of space was written on in huge, colorful letters, layer on top of layer, which should have looked cheerful. Instead it was menacing somehow, like a silent mob hanging there on the walls, waiting to jump out and get me. There were no benches or garbage cans or anything at all, just the closed-down token booth with its grilled window and the tiled walls, all scribbled over with spray paint.

I was shaking, literally shaking, but I made myself walk along the platform, looking for some sign of Joel.

There was nothing.

A train was coming. They pass through this station, they just don't stop anymore. When I was little I used to think it was a ghost station because it's so faintly lit. From the train it's just a glimpse, gone in an instant.

I ducked behind the curve in the wall by the stairs so I wouldn't be seen. The train roared by, the air pushed at me. Then it got quiet again.

"Joel!" I yelled.

Somewhere down in the tunnels something answered. I heard a faint sound, a greedy, gabbling, chuckling noise, snarling and gnashing and coming closer. The lights started to go very dim. Wrapped in darkness, I thought, in a panic. *Bound* in darkness. Already I could barely see.

I turned and ran up the steps mostly by feel, my fingers scrabbling at the dirty concrete. In my head I was screaming, I'm lost, I'm lost, though I had no breath to say anything out loud.

I was grabbed by the arms and pulled up onto the sidewalk, and the grate banged shut. Paavo walked me away down Broadway with his arm around my shoulders, holding me steady, keeping me on my feet. Behind us papers scuttered aimlessly to a halt as the little wind died down.

Nobody even looked at us. New York.

I staggered along next to Paavo, still shaking. "Joel's gone," I said. "We're too late. The kraken must have eaten him and now it's going to eat everything. What'll we do?"

"Got a little money?" he said.

I had the new week's allowance. Of course with his fiddle broken and the replacement with Joel, Paavo had no way to make any money for himself. Some magician. "What do we need money for?" I said crankily.

"We're going to go see your Granny Gran."

11
Water Magic

We caught a bus down to the Port Authority Bus Terminal and we went into the rest rooms there and got cleaned up a little. We were both pretty grubby from the Ninety-first Street station.

I bought us tickets to New Jersey. While we waited for the bus, I phoned the nursing home and asked if I could drop in on Granny Gran, and they said sure. When I went back to wait for the bus with Paavo, he had a cigarette hanging out of the corner of his mouth.

He half-offered me the pack again, he was that preoccupied. He remembered before I declined.

"Good," he said. "It's a lousy habit."

"Why don't you just magic it away?" I said.

He took the cigarette out of his mouth and looked at it. "I like it," he said. "Anyhow, it doesn't hurt to keep in mind what it feels like to have a lousy habit that you enjoy too much to change."

"Are you okay?" I asked him. He looked dead tired.

"What about you?" he countered, and I realized that *I* was dead tired, too. "One thing about magic, it takes it out of you, you know? It doesn't come for free. I'm out right now, I can't do anymore. So we'll go see what your granny

108

can suggest. I didn't want to bother her, but I got no choice left."

"You know her from Sorcery Hall?" I said.

He just nodded and puffed on his smoke. I got the feeling that he really didn't want to talk about that, so I didn't push it. We didn't talk about anything. I snoozed most of the way on the bus, I was so pooped.

From the bus stop, it was a short walk to the home. We found Granny Gran sitting out on the back lawn. The place was a big old rambling mansion, rickety but clean, and very quiet. A couple of staff people were on the porch, supervising a crewel class or something. Granny Gran was by herself, waiting for us.

Whenever I go to see her, I always worry that she'll look at me with that bright, desperate, friendly look that means she wants to know who I am but she doesn't. I didn't want her to be, well, senile in front of Paavo, especially when he seemed to be counting on her to help us find Joel and the key.

She didn't even look at me. She looked at Paavo and she put her hand out to him. He took it in both of his and just held it for a minute.

I cleared my throat. "Gran, this is—"

"I know who it is, Vee," she said. "It's good to see you," she said to him.

"Yah, Sarah Elizabeth," he said, "it's good."

God. He really knew her name, her whole name, which made her suddenly seem like somebody else, not just my Granny Gran.

"Sit down," she said.

I ran and got him a chair from the porch. I sat on the grass myself. It made me feel less like an intruder.

You know how you get twitchy when grown-ups are being moony about each other, because it's so gross? Even in the movies, the love stuff makes me squirm.

Well, this was different. I knew they were, well, attracted, I don't know. There it was between them left over from a time when they'd been more than attracted, I don't know. There it was between them without anybody making a big thing of it, and it was—not gross but awesome: for them to be so old and so still and so completely concentrated on each other like that, without having to say or do a single thing about it, except holding hands. Awesome.

Then Granny Gran said, "So, Paavo, what have you been doing to get all wrung out like this?"

"You know something about it already, don't you?" Paavo said. "You got a kraken here, you got guardian trouble."

They started talking about markers and guardians— the pyramids, some weird stone up in Iceland someplace, the chiming clock at the Central Park Zoo—

I laughed. "That's just a toy," I said.

Paavo shook his head. "That's what people think. And that's how you get in this kind of trouble. You lost a powerful control point when your people ripped down the old, what was it you called it? Penn Station, that was it."

"But you can't just keep all old things around forever!"

"No," he said, "but if people paid attention to something besides quick bucks, they'd have a sense of how to put up some new things to balance the loss of something old like that. Even half-asleep, your people sometimes do good protective things. As a rule, there's always power in anything that's been made with enough love to put beauty in it. New or old, that's the same."

"Boy," I said, "my art teacher would love to hear that!"

"Isn't that what he tries to teach you?" he said.

"Speaking of art and love, did you bring any short-cake?" Granny Gran said, and my heart sank. Whenever she lost the thread of the conversation she'd ask about shortcake, which I sometimes remembered to bring but not often, because she'd just taste it and tell me in triumph that it wasn't any good, nobody made decent shortcake these days.

"No shortcake till later," Paavo said, with a smile. He didn't smile often, I realized then. It was a pretty terrific smile, crinkly and warm. "We got work to do, Sarah Elizabeth, you know that. Can you help us find Joel and the key to the blue wall?"

Granny Gran said, "Did you know, Vee, that most true musicians would be candidates for some level or other of Sorcery Hall if they knew about it? Joel will be all right, if he survives the kraken."

"Where is he?" I said. "I looked in the Ninety-first Street station, but he was already gone!"

"He was never there," she said. "The kraken made a make-believe station, designed after that abandoned one, and put it someplace in the system. You'll have to find it and then get the key from the boy. You'll have to leave him there, though."

"Ah," Paavo said. "I was afraid of that. We can't get him out?"

"No, I don't think you can. But his chances of getting out on his own, once the kraken is defeated, are good—as long as he's got your bow, Paavo. He has some talent, he'll find a way to use it. Your job is to get the key. But not you, Paavo. You have to conserve your strength for the end. You hear me, Paavo Latvela? I'm looking at you, and I'm seeing a worn-out old man. You *must* rest. Vee will have to find Joel, get the key from him, and bring it to you."

Paavo shook his head. "Too dangerous."

"What choice do you have?" Granny Gran said.

"Find him how?" I said, my mouth all dry.

"Go into the subway and look for him," she said. "I'm sorry, Vee. It is dangerous. But I can't go, and Paavo mustn't. That leaves you."

Paavo started digging in his pockets for his cigarettes, still frowning. "Hell," he said.

I remembered what I'd heard in the abandoned station, that awful bubbling, jittering sound, flooding nearer and nearer with the speed of something in a nightmare.

I said, "Maybe the kraken will just go away by itself and let Joel go, if we wait. Maybe it'll get bored or find out it doesn't like it here as much as it thought."

Granny Gran said, "Haven't you been reading the papers, Vee?" She recited, in this calm voice, the things that had been happening. "Yesterday some workmen in a subway tunnel between Forty-second and Thirty-fourth streets were attacked by something they couldn't see. They were nearly driven into the path of an oncoming express. A woman had her legs scalded by a jet of steam from one of the gratings over some subway tracks. Another grating collapsed and dropped a couple of young men through the sidewalk. They haven't been found and won't be found. Motion like an earthquake has been felt in the basement of Bloomingdale's, opening cracks in some of the bearing walls."

"It tried to get me," I said. "At Ninety-first Street."

"It did," Paavo agreed grimly. "I smelled it."

Granny Gran said, "It's already got Joel and Joel's got the key. Without that key, we're all lost."

"How am I supposed to find him?" I said. "There are miles and miles of subways!"

Granny Gran said, "Hush now, here comes Mrs. Dermott."

Mrs. Dermott was one of the staff people. She came over smiling and said how nice it was of me to come to see Granny Gran and to bring an old friend of hers, too, which Paavo was, of course, but not in the way she thought. If she said anything to my mom about my showing up here with some old guy . . . funny thing to be thinking about, when I was supposed to be thinking about whether or not I would help save the world from the kraken! I was going to come out of this with some kind of weird permanent double vision. If I came out of it. If any of us did.

Mrs. Dermott seemed about to settle down and talk with us—I think she was curious about Paavo—but

Granny Gran said, "Would you go and see if you can find us some shortcake, dear? I have nothing on hand to offer my guests, and it isn't nice."

Mrs. Dermott winked at me and said she would. She left us alone.

"So, Valentine?" Paavo said. "What do you think?"

I looked at them: my white-haired old granny who in fact had hair so thin you could see her pink scalp through it, and Paavo with his face stamped full of lines and his wilted shirt collar open at his leathery throat and the cigarette hanging out of his mouth as if he were a gangster in a foreign movie.

Where were the crystal castles and flying dragons and crumbly old maps and terrific feasts and war horns whooping? No golden goblets of magical wine, no prophetic legends, no princesses in gorgeous embroidered cloaks. No stalwart prince to be our champion, victorious as foretold ages before.

Just me in my jeans with the black smears all over from being in the abandoned station; and Paavo with his violin smashed; and Granny Gran telling us what to do in one breath and asking for shortcake in the next; and my mom fluctuating like the tides with the fortunes of her love life; and Mrs. Dermott up on the porch, stopping to chat with some little old ladies who were playing cards and quarreling in high, birdie voices.

I took a deep breath. "What do I have to do?"

Paavo sighed and brushed ashes off his pants. Granny Gran sat staring off at the sky and picking at the blanket across her knees for a minute.

Then she said, "Ride the subway trains. In the tunnels between the real stations, look for the phantom station. No one will be able to see it but you. Then, Vee, you're going to have to slip off the end of the nearest platform and walk down the tunnel to Joel and get the key from him. I'm sorry, there's just no other way to do it that I can think of. Once you've got it, bring it to Paavo."

After a minute—he still didn't like the idea, I could see that—Paavo sighed again and said, "Come look for me at the Eighty-first Street station by the park."

"But the kraken," I croaked. "The Princes!"

"You leave them to us," Granny Gran said. "Between us, Paavo and I will make sure the enemy are kept busy while you're in their territory."

She sounded strange—eager, even. It occurred to me that maybe she was crazy.

"Oh boy," I said, kind of wobbly. I was really scared.

"Listen, Vee," Granny Gran said, "there's one thing we can do to make your part easier. Come over here."

She peeled back the blanket and started to get out of her chair, very shakily. Paavo jumped up and offered her his arm, and we went very slowly and unsteadily to the birdbath, which was a stone basin on a post. Granny Gran nodded to Paavo, and he wrote on the water with his finger, and there was Joel, slumped against the wall with his arms folded and his head pillowed on them. I think maybe he was crying, because his shoulders were moving a little.

Granny Gran said, "Open your thoughts, Vee. Paavo and I have a message for Joel. Slacken your mind and let us use it, and when I tell you to, put your finger on the image in the water."

I pulled back a little. I was nervous about touching the water after Paavo had put magic in it. I said, "I'm no magician."

"Shaa," Paavo said, and he reached over and slowly spread two fingertips outward from the center of my forehead above my eyebrows. All the tightness there went away. I felt my jaw go loose, which was a nice, sleepy feeling. Then Granny Gran nudged my elbow, and I let my hand glide over the surface of the water in the birdbath and then drop, like the tone arm of a phonograph, so that I just touched the reflection of Joel in the shallow water.

A sort of current ran up my arm and made me jump, and the quietness was all gone out of me again.

But the circles in the water spread and the surface got still again, and I saw Joel straighten up and lean the back of his head against the wall behind him where it said in huge letters, SHAZAM KID. Then, while the three of us watched, he felt along the edges of his violin case, opened the catches, and took out the fiddle and the bow—Paavo's bow. He began to tune the strings. Then he stood up and he played.

I couldn't hear anything, but I saw him playing and I saw his face become calm and concentrated. Then a twig dropped into the water from the tree hanging over us, and the image was gone.

"Listen," Granny Gran said to me. "Listen in the subway, and you'll hear him."

I said, "It sounds crazy to me, but I'll do it."

"Right away," Granny Gran said. "You only have tomorrow."

So it was that close. I no more thought to doubt Granny Gran's estimation of the time we had than to doubt the greenness of the grass around us. I couldn't believe how serene she looked, how calm her creased little face was, saying such a thing: you only have tomorrow.

Paavo said, "Yah, we better get going. I'm sorry we had to bother you."

"Oh, it's no bother," she said. "A person likes to think she can still do a little something, you know. But next time, Andy, please bring me some new pictures of the children. If you can't get them to come with you to this glum old place, at least bring pictures."

She thought he was my dead uncle Andy, and she turned to me and said, "I have something for you, Emma." My cousin Emma who lived in Sweden.

"I'm Vee, Granny," I said.

"Of course you are. No, I don't want to sit—as long as you two have me on my feet, help me to my room, will you? No use wasting all that effort."

I didn't want Paavo to see her room, not because it was ugly or anything—she had a nice room, small but bright and neat—but because I always hated to go in there on account of the smell. Not that it smelled bad, exactly, but there was this faint, dusty scent overlaid with perfume that I knew was the smell of being really old. I guess I wanted to avoid that for all of us.

Granny Gran insisted. So in we went, inching along at her pace, crowding into the little elevator, and shuffling down the hall to her room. People in the other rooms and along the hallways stared after us. I guess they had nothing live to look at most of the time that they hadn't seen a million times before, and they liked to gossip. Granny Gran told me once: "Little else to do, lovie, in these places, pleasant as they may be."

We sat her in the armchair by her window, at her direction, and then she took off a key she wore on a chain around her neck. "We do have our little security problems even here," she sighed. She opened a drawer in the desk under the windowsill. "I have something here for you, Vee."

She put into my hand one of those old change purses made of tiny steel links that you mainly see in antique clothing stores. It was bulging and heavy. I opened it and found it stuffed with silver dollars.

"But Granny," I said, hot-faced with greed and embarrassment at the same time, "I can't take your money!"

"Better now when you can use it than later when it doesn't matter, if there is a later," she said. "What are the fares these days, anyway—is it a dollar yet to ride the subway?"

So I gave her a big but careful hug, and Paavo took her bony little shoulders in his big hands and rested his cheek on hers for a minute, and we left. Mrs. Dermott met us at the door and thanked me again, and told me to tell my mom how well Granny Gran was doing. She kept looking at Paavo, though, with this bright, curious look.

We got out of there and caught a bus back to the city, not talking much. We were tired.

At the Port Authority, Paavo said, "You better not go home alone, Val."

"Why not?" I said belligerently. Frankly, I'd had about enough of being scared out of my wits for a while.

He shrugged. "That's how it feels to me," he said.

He came with me.

It was a good thing. The three Princes of Darkness were playing stoopball across the street from my building.

12
Hiding Out

We heard them before we saw them whooping and howling and jumping around like little kids. It's even possible that to Alec, the afternoon doorman, they actually did look like little kids, rowdy maybe, but harmless.

I couldn't guess how it would look to Alec when they grabbed me and Paavo to drag us off to the kraken.

We peeked at them from around the corner of my block.

"They think they're so smart," I whispered. "I can slip in through the Fudge."

Paavo growled back, "No. They know about that. It's underground, remember? A basement passage. The kraken knows, and what the kraken knows, they know. Go in now and you don't come out again. They'll trap you like a fly in a bottle."

And leave him alone out here without anyone to help him at all.

We got out of there as fast as we could. It was already late on that Saturday afternoon, and the chill in the air really cut.

"Where can I go?" I said.

"Well," he said, "you can't ride the subways alone at night to look for Joel, it's too dangerous. You got to wait and start tomorrow. Meantime, I know some places where we can rest."

We went to the library on Forty-second Street and took turns snoozing at the big tables in there, one of us reading and waking the other if a guard came by. It's a big, airy place full of quiet and dim light. You can sleep pretty soundly there if the guards let you.

Also this gave us a chance to do some research on the subways. I looked at plans and drawings and photographs until I was dizzy. Of course, some of the most important stuff listed in the catalogue was missing. It always is. People rob that place blind all the time. But we found enough for me to get a pretty good idea of the ground I was going to have to cover to locate the phantom station, and how a person is supposed to walk in the tunnels—avoiding the third rail and using the recesses in the walls to stand in when a train goes by—for when I would have to go in and get the key.

All the time I was doing this I had an unreal feeling. Me, go ride the trains down where the Princes hung out, by myself, with the kraken on watch for me in the noisy dark? And then I was going to actually *walk into the tunnels?*

Worst of all, I could see that no way in the world was I going to be able to get myself *and* somebody else who was blind back out of there. Supposing I could find Joel, and supposing next that I could get to him, Granny Gran was still right: I would have to take the key and leave him.

I concentrated on learning about the subway lines, especially the ones I wasn't familiar with. One thing I did not want to do was to get myself lost down there.

At six o'clock they closed the library.

I got us some dinner at Chock Full o' Nuts, and then we went to Grand Central and slept there for a while. We didn't look real ratty, like most of the derelicts. But I can tell you, I felt terrible. I mean, Paavo knew about these places because he'd had to use them, like any poor old bum, when he should have been treated like a terrific hero who had come to help us against a terrible threat. He had gray stubble on his cheeks now, but I knew that by nature he was neat as a cat—he didn't get a spot on him until he had to lift that grate at Ninety-first Street—and he shouldn't have had to sit around in the same clothes all the time and sleep in public places.

Well, nobody should, I guess. It was embarrassing, having him find my gran tucked away in even a nice old folks home, and now to see the benches at the Port Authority Bus Terminal (where we spent that evening) loaded for the night with poor old men and women with no place else to go. There were bag ladies washing themselves when I went into the rest room. I mean bathing piece by piece and changing their clothes. We have two bathrooms in our apartment, one for Mom and one for me.

Paavo and I sat and watched the pimps waiting around to see if any kids came off the buses, brand new to New York and easy prey. I had to explain that to Paavo. He didn't say anything. I had the feeling he'd seen that and worse in his life.

We only got really hassled once, but it was a sort of double whammy and it shook me up.

A guy in cowboy boots and a fringed vest fell into step with me on my way back from the ladies room. He had a really suave line: "Hey, bitch," he said, in this conversational tone, "you need a ride someplace?"

"No," I said, walking faster, but he kind of leaned toward me as we walked—he was telling me he thought I sure did need a ride and he had this car outside that I wouldn't believe—and I found myself herded into a corner.

I couldn't yell for help, not if it might lead to questions being asked about Paavo and me. I knew I was in trouble.

"Uh, listen," I said, "I have to get back to my uncle over there. He's waiting for me. He's a cop," I added in desperation. Dumb.

The leather creep laughed. "Oh yeah? Direct wheelchair traffic in the old folks homes, or what? What you hanging out with a old jerk like that for anyways? Bet he don't got a car, not even a scooter, not even a pair of *skates*."

A voice behind him whined, "Where's my soda? You said you'd bring me a soda. I'm still waiting."

It was Paavo, blinking and complaining like a crochety old grampa.

The leather creep glared at him over his shoulder. "Beat it, zombie," he said.

Paavo suddenly started to sing in this awful, quavery voice: "Casey would waltz with the strawberry blonde, and the band played on!" Heads turned. He was singing pretty loudly. "He held his girl in a strawberry whirl, and the band played on!"

The leather creep swore furiously under his breath and snarled at me, "Shit, if he wants you that bad, the senile old drooler can have you!" and he stomped away.

I think people like that really can't stand to feel ridiculous. I was red in the face myself.

Paavo and I went back to our seats, which luckily had not been taken by anybody else. We sat down.

"God," I said. I was sweating.

But we weren't in the clear yet.

A policewoman sat down on the other side of me. "You folks all right?" she said to me.

"Uh-huh," I said. "We're fine."

"Waiting for somebody?" she said, looking past me at Paavo. He had his eyes shut. This one was up to me.

"Um, yes, ma'am."

"Is your friend all right?"

I said, "He's my great-uncle Mike. I'm kind of staying with him to help out while Great-aunt Jill's in the hospital. But he misplaced his keys and we're locked out. My cousin Rita's coming with a spare set of keys as soon as she gets off her shift, out in Jersey."

Wow. Don't ask where in Jersey or a shift as what, please.

"Couldn't you get the neighbors to help out?" the lady cop said, still watching Paavo.

I leaned nearer to her to block her view of him, because I thought she might notice something if she looked long enough, something about him that would tell her he was special. I lowered my voice. "The neighbors are a little annoyed with him, actually, because he sings like that a lot. I think maybe a lady down the hall from him helped his keys disappear, you know what I mean? Revenge."

She looked at me now, and I thought, oh boy, you've gone too far. I sat there trying to look one hundred percent innocent. If she asked me for some ID—if my mom had reported me missing—

The cop stood up. "If you need anything, I'm around," she said, and she walked away.

I just sat there, contemplating the edge we somehow had not dropped over. If she'd asked *him* for some ID—!

Without opening his eyes, Paavo said, "Valentine, you're sure a fancy liar. I hope you never get carried away by your talent."

"You're a *terrible* singer," I hissed. "Where did you *get* that song?" 'Strawberry whirl' sounds like an ice-cream flavor!"

"I forgot that part so I had to make it up," he said. "Is she gone? Good. Come on."

We walked eastward, away from dirty old Eighth Avenue.

I said, "I guess she was just trying to protect me, you know? She thought you were—" Now how was I going to tell him she probably had figured I was in the clutches of a mole-ster or worse?

"I know what she thought," he said.

"I'm sorry."

"I'm not," he said firmly. "I'm glad she took an interest. Maybe sometime she'll help some other kid that needs it. You got a mean world here, Valentine, that devours its stray children."

"What would we have done if she hadn't believed me?" I said. You know how when the danger's more or less past, you like to wallow in how bad it might have been.

"Whatever we could," Paavo said. He was not a wallower.

"Was that a magic song? 'Strawberry Whirl'?"

"I learned it a long time ago from your Granny Gran. That's the only magic in it."

I looked up at the sky. You can't see the stars well at night in New York because there's so much light from the city, but you can make some of them out if you let your eyes get adjusted. Not that night. It was cloudy. I said, "Paavo, what star do you come from? What planet?"

"This planet," he said, sounding surprised. "But long ago. I forgot how long. I forgot how it is here. Money, for one thing. And I forgot how I would have to be, coming back here now."

Old, he meant. So in Sorcery Hall he looked different: younger. I didn't pursue that. I liked the way he was now, I liked him as I knew him.

We sat down on the steps outside the entrance to Bryant Park. The park was locked, so nobody could come up behind us. Outside we could see anyone coming up on us, cops or whoever.

"Paavo," I said, "what is Sorcery Hall, exactly?"

"Oh, it's like a club," he said, "a professional association. The members come from all over, you know, to learn from each other and work together on projects."

"What kind of projects?"

"Keeping worlds like yours out of trouble, for one thing. You had some knowledgeable people here in some earlier cycles of your history." Like himself, I guessed. Maybe he'd been a Druid, or something even earlier that nobody knows about anymore. I was shy about asking, so I didn't. He went on, "Some of them are still keeping an eye on you now that it's all youngsters here. I mean young spirits. Mostly we try not to interfere because you only learn by taking care of your own problems, but a kraken— well, that's a little more than you can handle without help."

"Well, where are you? I mean, is it an actual place called Sorcery Hall?"

"It's just on a different plane from this one, that's all, a sort of level where we like to get together and keep in touch."

"How many of you?"

"Depends."

"Why can't you get help from there? I mean somebody stronger and smarter than I am to help you?"

"We didn't realize how serious it was, or you can bet I'd have come prepared better." He sounded really grim. "Your message was general, you know what I mean? It wasn't clear what you had on your hands here. Now I know, but you got so much static coming off the kraken, I can't get through. And in Sorcery Hall they don't know how to get through to me without maybe doing more damage here than the kraken itself wants to do."

"So it's just us?"

"It's just us."

Thing about Paavo, he never faked it. I would have liked him to have faked that particular part just then, but I guess it was better that he didn't.

There was a taint in the air, a little like what you get when there's a garbage strike in the city: rot. I was restless. We got moving again.

We walked along Madison Avenue eating hot dogs I got us at some corner joint. One thing about sleeping out like that, you wake a lot and you notice that you haven't eaten since dinner and you get hungry. I still had some allowance money, so we didn't have to dig other people's garbage out of the trash cans to eat, like real street people do. I was very glad I could spare Paavo that, though I knew if he had to do it he would, and no fuss.

We were coming up to a row of pay phones. I thought about stopping to phone my mom and reassure her, but it occurred to me that she might have the police all ready to trace the call. Besides, what could I tell her? Don't worry, Mom, I'm sleeping out tonight with an old wizard from another plane, and tomorrow I go down into the kraken's territory? Great. I kept walking.

"How did Granny Gran get to be a member of Sorcery Hall?" I said.

"She was a natural," Paavo said. "You got a lot of wild talent here. We noticed her because she was doing the kind of crude work that can get dangerous if you really don't know what you're doing. So we contacted her. She learned fast. It was a loss to us when she retired."

We went over to Lexington, walking slowly in the chilly, quiet night. I felt danger all around us. Maybe

because we'd already come through some danger together, I was more sensitive to it. It was funny, I wasn't as
scared as I should have been. Being in trouble along with
somebody you absolutely trust is different from just being
terrified. It's a strange feeling, to be happy at the same time
you're in danger and you're a little cold and a lot tired. Not
happy, exactly: more like contented, which is pretty weird.
But I liked it. I liked us looking out for each other, walking
around tired and grubby in the night.

A cab came rocketing up the empty avenue and
Paavo yanked me away from the curb. The cab kept
going, and he kept his hand on my shoulder. I knew what
he was thinking: suppose the Princes had been in that cab,
ready to snatch me right off the street?

There really was nobody else to help us. We were in
this on our own.

13
Trust

It got to me, I guess, a little after that, when we passed a station of the East Side subway on Lexington. All of a sudden my skin turned cold and I started to cry.

"What?" said Paavo, stopping and turning me so he could look in my face. "What is it?"

"Paavo, I can't go into the subway again. I'm scared the kraken and the Princes will get me."

I felt as if I'd said magic words. It was time for him to smile and tell me the test was over, that he was bringing in a whole army from Sorcery Hall. Thanks to me and Granny Gran, he and his professional association of wizards would handle the kraken themselves.

Frankly, I just wanted to go home and crawl into my bed and let my mom yell until she was tired and live with that until it went away. Just to be done with it all, out of it, and safe.

Paavo said, "Shaa. Val. You'll be okay."

"I can't," I said. "I don't know anything about this kind of stuff. I'm not a fighter, Paavo."

"Oh?" he said, walking on. "What about getting down to the store and back again with groceries and the change, in spite of the mean kids on the corner? What about every day going past Mr. Carneros's dog that you

130

were scared would jump out of its yard and chew your leg off? What about when those kids in school tried to take your allowance from you when you walked in the door, and you got the basketball team after them?"

"Hey," I said, "wait a minute. Those are private and personal things from when I was younger. You can't bring them up now. They have nothing to do with this."

He said, "I'm just reminding you, you're not as sheltered as you think. This city, this world—they don't encourage survival except for tough people like you, Val."

I said, "But we're talking about walking out along the subway tracks. I bet they didn't even have subways when you were around here last. You just don't understand. If you grow up here, you get told from the time you're two feet high that one of the things you never, never do is walk on the subway tracks. It's for good reasons, even when you don't have a kraken after you."

"True," he said. He shoved the curly hair off his forehead with the back of his wrist.

"I can't," I said.

He nodded. "Okay."

I was so surprised that I didn't say anything for a block.

"'Okay'?" I said finally. "What do you mean, 'okay'?"

A shrug.

"I want to know what that means, Paavo."

"I'll figure out something."

Which meant that he would go into the subway himself. Without resting, without his magic fiddle, without even his bow, which Joel still had.

Well, Paavo was a grown-up, and this was his job. Probably he could do a lot better than I could.

We walked. He coughed and pulled out his cigarettes. I saw his face when he bent over the match flame: creased, tired, dark around the eyes. Patient. He had known all along that I couldn't be counted on. No, he'd hoped I would do it, but he knew better than to depend on me. But he wasn't going to make me feel bad for letting him down.

On the other hand, he was obviously just too tired to put on a show of casual good humor about it.

Too tired.

"Okay," I said miserably. "I'll do it. I'll find Joel, and I'll get the key and bring it to you at Eighty-first Street."

He pressed my shoulder. "Good," he said.

Sometime later on he shuffled me out of the all-night movie house we were trying to sleep in and down to the new Penn Station, where we finished the night. I woke up feeling cramped and smelling something sharpish and stale, and feeling that it was late. The smell was that tobacco stink that smokers carry with them. For an instant I thought it was my mom. She never smoked but people at her office did, and she always came home scented with burnt tobacco.

I opened my eyes.

Well, of course it wasn't her. It was Paavo, sitting next to me on a bench.

"Have I overslept?" I said. It was Sunday morning and the waiting room echoed with people to-ing and fro-ing.

"I let you sleep," he said. "You don't go kraken-running without plenty of sleep."

"You make it sound like walking the dog!"

"The dog that ate the world," he said, wrinkling his nose as if he smelled something bad.

"Can it really do that?" I said. "The kraken? How can it do that if it's small enough to fit under New York?" Which wasn't exactly my idea of small, but even New York kids learn after a while that the world is one heck of a lot bigger than their city.

"Oh, it starts pretty modest," he said. "But it could grow very big and fast, using a town like this one for an appetizer."

"Hey, I dreamed about Joel!"

The dream was clear in my memory: there was Joel, reaching out of this drinking fountain in the park to pull me into the water where he was, perfectly dry and very jittery and excited. He held onto my hand and talked very fast and anxiously to me. He said I had to get him out of there quickly. He was playing music to keep sane and because it seemed to make the kraken angry. "I can hear it thrashing around in the tunnels," he said, "and sometimes it stinks so bad I can hardly breathe. What you smell gets pretty important when you can't see anything." He couldn't see, of course, because he had taken off his scarf and tied it around his eyes, and sure enough, there was the red mark on his neck, the fiddler's brand.

I was scared, in the dream, to hear that his playing was stirring up the kraken, but I couldn't tell him to stop. "Keep playing, Joel," I said. "It's the only way I have of finding you."

He grinned and squeezed my hand and was all of a sudden a very likable person, a person I cared about a lot. "Like Richard the Lion-Hearted finding Blondel," he said, and I laughed and said it was the other way around, but he went right on. "Don't sing. Go fishing."

He let go of my hand and started using Paavo's bow like a fishing rod, as if he were casting an imaginary line. End of dream.

I told it all to Paavo.

"Funny thing to dream," I said. "Blondel and Richard the Lion-Hearted! That's just a myth anyway, isn't it?"

"I don't know," he said. "Who's Richard the Lion-Hearted?"

I have to admit I was a little shocked at his ignorance, until I realized that probably while we were having Richard the Lion-Hearted, Paavo was off saving some other planet from a kraken or worse. I liked being the one to explain something to him for a change.

"Richard the Lion-Hearted was an English king who led the Crusades, and one of his enemies, the King of Austria I think, grabbed him while he was heading home across Europe and locked him up in some dungeon someplace. Nobody knew where Richard was, to ransom him. His minstrel, Blondel, found him by wandering around Europe singing outside prison windows until King Richard answered him. Bet you the song was 'Strawberry Whirl.'"

As I said that, I had the funniest feeling—a terrible sadness just rushed up in me as I sat there smiling at Paavo.

Because I realized that when we beat the kraken, it was all going to end. Our adventure, our partnership, our kidding around, everything. Paavo had come here to do this particular thing. When it was over, he wouldn't stay around. Why should he be an old street musician in our world when he belonged in Sorcery Hall as a great wizard? Would I even ever suggest anything like that? I could want it, I could want it really badly, but I couldn't say so. At least I didn't have to try and work out the mechanics—explaining him and the kraken to my mom, for instance. Because no way in the world could I ask Paavo to settle for what he could do and be here, just so he would stay around and be my friend.

Maybe later on he'd drop in once in a while to say hello or something, if I was lucky, if he had a little time; if I even remembered and believed my own memories when I got older. Maybe now and then I'd hear violin music on some street corner someplace and I'd hurry to see and find him there, just stopping by to make sure things are all right. But in general my life in our world-without-wizards was not seriously going to include him, that was all.

"I think it's just a story," he said.

"What is?" I said. I kept staring at him because a time was coming when he wouldn't be there, and boy, did that hurt.

"Richard the Lion-Hearted and Blondel," he said patiently. He tapped my forehead with his knuckle. "Hey, how you doing in there? Anyway, from your dream it sounds like Joel is ready. So, what about you? How do you feel?"

That brought me down hard from whatever cloudy place I'd been: I had to get started, if I still meant to. It was just like Paavo to ask me again, to give me another chance to say no.

I stalled a little: "You mean, have I changed my mind about going into the subway?"

"That's right."

I thought about it, feeling the beginning of fear all mixed up with hunger for breakfast, and then suddenly I started to laugh.

"Hey, Paavo." I said, "I don't have to walk in the tunnels! I don't have to go into the subway at all! I'm just supposed to bring the key out, right?"

"That's the important part, yah," he said.

"Well, if Joel is playing music, I can find him from the street, through the subway ventilation gratings. I can get the key, too, from up above. Joel told me how."

I explained to Paavo how city kids go fishing: you get a long string and some gum you've chewed that's good and sticky, and you tie something small and heavy to the end of the string to weight it and you stick the gum to the weight. Then you lower the whole thing through a street grating and try to get the gum to stick to and pick up coins that you imagine have fallen out of the pockets of people walking over the grating. You never catch anything much, but it's a good game if you pretend there's all kinds of treasure coming up from down there.

"The key's the treasure," I said. "All I have to do is locate the grating over the phantom station. The kraken wouldn't make a station without all the street grilles over it, would it?"

Paavo scratched the mark on his neck. "They don't invent, they only imitate, and they do that pretty good. There's probably a grating, but listen, it won't open like the one over the real closed-down station. Otherwise Joel might be able to escape, blind or not. The grille will just be window-dressing, you know what I mean? You can't get Joel out through there, only the key, if this works."

"It'll work, it'll work!" I said, really excited. "The gratings over the Broadway line are right above the stations. You can look in and see the trains go by underneath. All I need is some string."

"But," he said, "it might not be so easy, Val. And you might still have to go underground at some point. Don't discount that."

"I'll chance it," I said. I was feeling great.

"Okay," he said. "How about something to eat? But we better go wash up a little first."

I went to the ladies room and cleaned up the best I could.

Looking in the mirror, I started to get all trembly. This was me, the me that Paavo saw when he looked at me: not some wimpy brat or a grade-school kid, but this person who was helping him fight the kraken.

I'd give him the key and he'd fix the kraken and then he'd go, and maybe that me would be gone too. Anyway, the one person I knew I could trust completely was going to leave me, and whose one-person-they-knew-they-could-trust-completely would *I* be then?

I guess I got pretty rattled, because when I came out I sat down next to him and I said, "Paavo, can I tell you something?"

"Sure."

"I think I love you." Oh God, did I really say that?

"Good," he said. Then he added, "I mean, good that you said it."

"You knew!" I squeaked, more horrified than before.

"Sure I knew. When you feel that pull toward another person—just here, right?" He tapped himself below the middle of the chest, under the breastbone: "Yah. That's what it is."

"You feel it too?" What if he did, what then? All of a sudden we were going way too fast for me.

"Sure I do," he said. "The other person always feels it, even if they pretend they don't."

"Oh," I croaked.

"Okay if I smoke?" he said. I nodded and he took the last bent cigarette from a rumpled package and lit up and blew smoke through his nose. "Val," he said, "your mother has ideas about love, yah?"

"Ideas?" I said. "She has whole lectures!"

"Okay, I have a lecture too. You want to hear it?"

"Yes," I said, not daring to look at him. Love? We were going to talk about love, me and this old wizard from another plane? What had I gotten myself into? I should have just gone charging off into the kraken's lair, it would have been easier.

"Here's what I think," he said. "Love is never bad, you understand? Complicated, maybe. Sometimes it's so tied up it can only *be,* it can't *do* anything. And sometimes that's plenty, and sometimes it's a damn good thing. I'm talking about love now, this kind." He touched the same spot on his chest again. "Not just appetite, or flirting, or mischief. This is the kind where what you want for the other person is what they want for themselves, whether *you* like it or not. You don't ever want to pretend that feeling isn't there when it is; or vice versa, either. That kind of faking can twist you up something terrible. So you always want to say to yourself, no, this isn't it; or yes, it is. And if it is, where you go from there, you got to make some careful choices."

"Choices?" I said. I was petrified of what he was going to say.

"For me, it's not to do anything to make us uncomfortable with each other, you and me. For you—whatever you decide, inside what my choice leaves."

I felt this dizzy rush of relief—he meant I was safe. But who did he think he was, anyhow, telling me what was left for me to decide after he decided?

Words rushed out of me: "You mean—I wasn't thinking—I couldn't, I wouldn't, you're so *old!*" And I wanted to die. Of course I'd had this fleeting thought of, well, us kissing and a sort of whirling, suffocating blank beyond that, and of course he knew, and now I'd said this awful thing.

He smiled and blew more smoke. "That's right," he said. "I am."

"It doesn't matter though," I gabbled, clutching the arm of the bench for dear life. "I mean, you're a magician, you can be any age you want and you could even change my age to match yours, couldn't you?" God, change my age? To what? To be old like my mother, like Granny Gran even? What was I *saying?*

"Sure I could change you," he answered. "Outside. Inside, no. I couldn't do that and still keep you yourself. And since it's yourself I love, I don't want to do that, do I?"

"But you could make yourself younger," I said. I couldn't help myself. I had this wild image of him changing himself into a kid right there in Penn Station and nobody even noticing. Except me. It's yourself I love, he'd said.

He shook his head. "I got nothing left to learn as a youngster. This is what I'm learning now." He slapped his own leg, an old man's leg, thin under the wrinkled, rust-colored corduroys. "I got lessons to do like this, and that's what I'm ready to do, so that's what I'm doing. I won't use magic to cut school, Val."

I giggled at the idea of Paavo in school, and the next thing I knew I was bawling like a little kid. I'd sort of asked him to stay with me after all, and he'd answered, and I couldn't help it, I cried.

If he'd patted me on the head, I would have expired right there. But he sat smoking, squinting one eye behind the smoke, and saying, "Shaa, Val, it's okay, take it easy," until I dried up.

Then he said, "Are you ready for breakfast? I want you to get something to eat, take your time, loaf around a while. About noon, you start looking for Joel; not before."

"Why?" I said. "We only have today, Granny Gran said. And what about you? What are you going to be doing?"

"Resting, getting set. I've got it worked out. Playing on the street, you meet people. Remember that guy who stopped to talk to me in the park that day, before we did some magic? He gave me ten dollars. He's a musician, and he invited me to stop by his place for coffee any Sunday. Him and some friends, they do chamber music just for their own pleasure, Sunday mornings until noon. You get breakfast. I'll go to his place and listen."

"Just listen to music?" I said. My heart was bonking away nervously at my ribs because we were so close to going our separate ways, which I wanted to put off as long as I could.

"Listen," he said, "maybe play a little on somebody's spare fiddle, eat some herring. He serves bagels and pick-led herring, he told me. And good strong coffee. I'll eat better than you will, and music is good for me.

"Afterward, I'll go to that little park with the waterfall on Fifty-third Street, you know the one? I got things to do that need plenty of moving water. It's going to take both of us, your Granny and me, to keep the kraken and the Princes occupied while you find Joel.

"I'll know when you've got the key, and I'll head for the Eighty-first Street station to meet you. It better be before sundown, Val. The dark helps the kraken. Be quick."

We went up on the sidewalk. It was cold out. A raw, dirty wind was sweeping paper scraps down the gutters, and the sky was a dull color.

He said, "Can you spare some money for cigarettes? I'm all out."

I divided the last of my allowance between us.

"Oh," he said, "wait a minute." He pulled a coil of thin cord out of his pocket and handed it to me. "For your fishing." God knows where he got it, and I didn't ask.

I said, "You'll be waiting for me at Jagiello's station?"

"Once you got the key, you head right there," he said. "But look, Val, if I don't come, and the sun sets, take the key downstairs yourself and open the door for Jagiello. No hesitation, no waiting around. Just do it, okay?"

"Why wouldn't you be there?" I said, feeling this sudden drench of fear.

"I got to figure out how to get Jagiello moving once he's free so he can go back where he belongs. He's only a statue, you know, a guardian. He was never meant for more than just standing there. It's different when all of a sudden you got to be a warrior, you got to pick up your big bronze feet and move. It might take longer than I think, making that work. I might be late. Listen, don't worry, okay? Either we do it, or we don't, that's all. What's to worry about in that? If we fail, no more worries for anybody."

"But you'll be there," I insisted, "when I show up at the station. You'll meet me."

"I plan to," he said. "Just if I don't, and the sun goes down, use the key. You're not Joel, you can do it. Don't wait."

He shoved back that stray swatch of hair that the wind kept tugging down over his eye.

"You want to borrow my comb?" I said, wishing like crazy that he would say yes. I wanted to give him something, anything of mine, before we headed in different directions.

"No, thanks," he said. "Don't they tell you in school never to lend your comb to people?" He smoothed his thick gray curls back with his palms. "Looks better?"

"Looks great," I said.

I had a powerful urge to give him the biggest hug in the world, but while I hesitated he put his hand out for me to shake. It was as if we both suddenly got a little shy, having spent the night together, so to speak. He turned my hand in his big, warm paw and kissed the back of it, and then he walked away with that neat, brisk step of his, his head up as if he was staring down anybody bigger than he was.

So much for the war horns and prophecies and unicorns and kings from my reading that I'd been missing in real life. It took me a while to work it out—I guess I'm kind of slow about some things—but I knew that morning that however things came out in the end, my honest-to-goodness rumpled old wizard who needed a shave and had to borrow money for cigarettes was worth more than that whole bunch of clichéd fantasy claptrap rolled up together.

14

Blondel

Scared as I was, I didn't have much appetite, but I managed to get through some waffles and sausages and a little orange juice, which left me with bus fare, that was all. I walked around the theater district looking at show posters for a while, read part of a Sunday *Times* somebody had dumped in a trash can—funny how that made me feel. All those dopes and fanatics busy gunning each other down all over the world were going to have to give it up for good if the kraken wasn't stopped.

At noon on the button I started my search for Joel.

I walked along the gratings above the subway tunnels. I had to carefully not think about the three Princes, for fear they would turn up, called somehow by my thoughts. I hoped like mad that they were completely occupied by Paavo's and Granny Gran's diversionary tactics.

But were there any diversionary tactics, or had something gone wrong? The kraken was certainly right there with me. Once, I think I caught a glimpse of it—a sort of oily, bubbling darkness rushing through a tunnel below me, with little chips of dirty red light sparkling in it. I smelled it all the time, and I heard it: a clatter and racket and rumbling came pouring up out of the gratings wherever I went. How would I ever hear Joel's violin?

It was getting colder and quieter out, the streets emptier, the traffic sparser. How much time did we really have?

I thought about going to the midtown waterfall park to find Paavo. But I didn't have the key yet. If he could have done without that, he would have. He wouldn't send me trudging through the city, constantly looking over my shoulder in case the three Princes were on my trail, for nothing.

It was so cold for spring, and I was only wearing a thin cardigan over my T-shirt and the jeans that I'd walked out of my house with yesterday—only yesterday? A day and a night—Mom would be frantic.

I stopped for a rest at Forty-second and Sixth, where at least some people were walking around.

A blind old beggar I'd seen before came stumping up the subway steps with her accordion in her arms. She wore a green wool hat and green socks. The rest of her was covered in tweed pants and a hairy checked coat. Granny Gran had said something about musicians being keyed into magic. Wasn't this a musician?

"Excuse me," I said.

She hugged her accordion tighter and kind of hunched against the railing, facing me. Maybe she expected to be robbed of whatever she'd made that morning bawling "Annie Laurie" at the top of her lungs to the music of her accordion in the subway cars.

I said, "Have you heard anybody playing the violin anyplace in the subway today?"

She cocked her head and seemed to be looking at me from these closed-down eye sockets with nothing in them. The tin can she wore wired to her coat belt was empty. I took out one of Granny Gran's silver dollars and dropped it in with a good, solid clink.

The beggar smiled. "Thanks, dear. Sure, there's somebody playing on the BMT line between the Fourteenth Street and Twenty-third Street stations. If he's a friend of yours, tell him he'll never make it unless he electrifies his violin and learns to play something popular."

I got on a downtown bus.

It broke down. I had to wait for another bus.

This one got stuck in traffic because of construction and double-parking. Then there was a collision with a delivery van. The third bus went slowly, but it went.

Finally I reached Twenty-third and got started on foot, and this part should have been easy: just find the subway gratings over the BMT line between Twenty-third and Fourteenth and follow them. Surely the kraken had lost track of me while I was traveling in the bus.

But when I did find a grating and stood looking down through it into the subway, what I heard wasn't Joel's violin but the kraken again. Not just its horrible multiple voices. Now there was a sound of big motion like someone in creaky leather armor flexing enormous muscles: a sort of heavy, dark, seething sound, and a scraping, dragging sound.

I reached Fourteenth Street without any luck, and I began to think that the kraken must have moved Joel and the phantom station again. I started working outward, east and west, block by block, listening at all the gratings in the sidewalk, which is a lot of gratings, most of them for deliveries into the basements of buildings. I was catching the kraken sound through any sidewalk grating at all now, and I began to panic.

Couldn't the kraken stick the phantom station in a basement instead of right on the subway line if it wanted? Suppose I had already passed Joel a couple of times and he just couldn't make himself heard over the noise of the kraken? Suppose I never heard him, never found him?

I was crying by then as I walked.

All of a sudden there was this blast from below, like a stream engine whooping. Those jibbery, fussing voices, like a flock of snaky birds pecking and climbing on each other, faded. The leathery noises ended. The subway seemed to be holding its breath down there.

Granny Gran and Paavo must have found some way to draw the kraken off.

Then I heard music, like a sad voice singing far away and without words. I ran along, pausing to listen at each grating, until I found the source.

Here: it was Joel's violin, of course. I squatted down beside a grille outside a closed-up travel agency. The music had turned spiky and snappish. All I could see below was what looked like train track, very dim and dusky, where no track should be. It was the phantom station.

I checked around quickly, and sure enough, the kraken had included the little square entrance grilles set into the street corners around the phantom station, just like at the real Ninety-first Street station on Broadway. But

as Paavo had warned me, the one that should open
wouldn't. The metal was real, all right: it cut into my fingers
when I pulled hard. But the grating wouldn't budge, and
anyway there were no dirty concrete steps under it, just a
blank, dark space. There was no way to bring Joel out.

I went back to the main grille over the pretend tracks. I
was scared to call Joel by name in case the kraken heard
and came tearing back. So I sang, sort of, over the furious
notes Joel was playing. I must have sounded awful, but I
had to be loud to be heard over the rage of the violin. What
the heck, I'd sung for Paavo in the park and hadn't died of
inadequacy because of it. It wasn't the opera.

I sang, "Here I am, I've come for the thing you have
for me. I'll drop down some string. Tie the something onto
it and I'll pull it up. I hope you're okay."

A woman with her arms full of packages walked by
and gave me a weird look. I gave her a weird look back.
She kept going.

The music stopped. I heard sounds of movement
below, and suddenly there was Joel, standing right on the
tracks, his face turned up to me. I knew he couldn't see me
by the way he was stretching his eyes as wide as he could.

He looked awful, white-faced and skinny, and I
wondered if he was getting anything to eat or drink down
there in his phantom prison. My night wandering around
with Paavo was suddenly more special than before: all that
time Joel had been stuck here, in the cold and the dark,
alone with nothing but his music to keep him company,
nothing but his fiddle to trust.

"Is it night up there?" he whispered. "I can't see you."

I whispered back, "Paavo says the kraken has wrapped you up in darkness to keep you here. There's nothing wrong with your eyes."

"I'm not worried," he said in this bitter voice, "there've been blind fiddlers in the world before. How are you going to get me out of here?"

"I can't."

"But you've got to!" he said, straining up toward me. "I can't do anything down here, I can't see! How can I fight the damned kraken like this?"

I explained about the string I was about to lower, weighted with a pack of gum I'd bought for the purpose.

"Forget that," he said. "Come get me, Tina!"

"I can't," I said, carefully feeding the weighted end of the string through the grating. I had the other end tied to my wrist, not to take any chances.

"You have to get me out of here!" He was practically screaming.

I said, "For God's sake, Joel, stop it! Are you crazy? We need the key!"

The bright yellow gum package turned and dangled above Joel's pale face. I waited, kneeling there, hardly able to breathe. Of all things, this was the least expected: that Joel wouldn't help, that Joel would refuse.

"He told you to leave me down here?" he demanded.

"There isn't any choice," I said. "Come on, hurry, will you?" The wind was digging at me and the sky was this heavy, sullen gray. I thought I could feel the entire sidewalk trembling a little, vibrating, getting ready to tear apart and collapse as the kraken returned to get us both. "You don't know what it's like up here—"

"You don't know what it's like down *here*," he said. "You don't know what's it's like to be stuck in the dark like a helpless, brainless baby while everybody else is out there fighting!"

"Please, Joel! Give me the key! What if the kraken comes back?"

All around was this tremendous stillness that falls on commercial parts of the city on Sundays when everybody's gone. That made it easier to listen for the return of the kraken.

Joel brushed the gum pack away where it had touched his cheek. Then he grabbed at it and pulled hard on the cord. "You didn't answer me," he said. "Paavo said to do this? To leave me here?" From the sound of his voice, he was almost crying.

"Nobody wants to, Joel. But we have to," I said.

Nothing

I said, "He said it, Joel. I'm sorry, it's how things are."

The string jiggled. He was working on it, without a word. I waited, listening for the kraken.

"Come on," I said.

He gave a tug on the string. He had taken off the gum and tied the key to the blue door on in its place. I drew it up. For a second the key stuck in the little square opening of the grating—the rounded part of the key was wider than the pack of gum had been—and I thought, if it's too big to pass through, what are we going to do? I took a deep breath and kind of eased and wiggled the key through, and there it was in my hand again, the little piece of metal that could defeat the kraken.

Maybe.

Down below Joel whispered, "It's so dark. What am I going to do?"

I said, "It'll be okay, now that I've got this," but I was thinking of black, greasy kraken smoke coiling around him and flying up to grab me. "Play Paavo's music, Joel. You have your violin, and you have Paavo's bow. Use them! The gum is for you, too. I've got to go now."

My watch had stopped. I didn't know what time it was, but it felt late. I was sure not going to take the subway uptown. I started trotting north.

There were no cabs, no buses, no nothing. The streets down here looked deep and black with shadow.

Jogging along, I could hear something, under my own breathing. It was a far-off, ugly sound, a chittering-grinding-growling-many-voices sound. It came pouring up out of the sidewalk gratings on a hot, dark wind. The kraken was coming back.

I turned sharply and headed over to Fifth Avenue so I wouldn't be right over the subway line. I settled down to run.

Megan and I have walked all the way from Battery Park, at the tip of Manhattan, to where we live on the Upper West Side. Once we even went as far as Columbia University, just for the heck of it. It's not so hard and it doesn't take so long, not if you swing your arms and move and if you don't stop and look at store windows or anything, and if you get the right rhythm so the traffic lights don't stop you at every corner.

The traffic lights were no problem for me now. They were all red. Around Thirty-fourth Street, drivers were screaming and honking their horns on the outskirts of a huge traffic jam. They were getting out of their cars to argue and complain.

"The goddamn trains," they said. "The goddamn traffic lights!" I caught enough to realize that the kraken—or something—had messed around with the underground electrical system so that the subways were not working at all and the traffic lights were all out of sync or jammed. No wonder the midtown streets were crazy with stalled traffic.

Every clock I saw, in a store window or outside a bank, was stopped at a different time.

My legs were aching from pounding along on concrete, even in my new running shoes. But with things the way they were, nothing was going to be able to carry me uptown faster than my own feet.

I ran.

At Forty-second Street I got a stitch in my side and I had to walk for a while. Then I ran again.

At Fifty-third the stitch came back but this time I did what they say you can do if you try: I ran through it.

At Fifty-ninth dirty gray steam billowed out of a grating two blocks away in a mean, hot cloud. I made a detour of an extra block.

The sky was dark and sort of streaming the way it looks before a hurricane. I kept thinking, the clouds are coming from down here, from underground. The kraken is trying to bring on night early so it can gush up into the streets and take over. What was sunset, after all? The actual time the sun dropped down past the horizon, or when it got dark out? The kraken was trying to cheat.

I didn't think at all about Joel, not rationally. I only hoped. Maybe now that I had the key the kraken would be so busy coming after me, it would forget about him. Joel would get away somehow, or maybe Paavo would go get him out. I didn't believe any of this for a minute, but I hoped.

The key was clutched in my fist. I pumped along, soaking with sweat and with my lungs hurting. The few people out on Central Park West under that sky turned to stare after me. I must have looked like the person carrying the news that World War Three was starting, which maybe in some weird way was going to be true if I didn't get to Paavo in time.

Up here I could try to get a cab, but I knew that something would happen if one did stop for me. A manhole lid would fly off under us and smash the cab's axle, a hunk of street would cave in and strand us, anything to keep me from getting to where I was going. If the kraken could tie up the traffic lights, it could surely do that. So I just stumped along, walking mostly because I could only run a few steps at a time now, I was so tired and achey.

I passed a couple of cops at Seventy-second Street. They were talking to each other and they didn't even see me shuffling along. What could I have said to them if they'd asked me what was wrong?

Past the museum, past the steep little park going down to the planetarium. There was the Eighty-first Street station.

It was dark and windy, after sunset by that standard anyway, and Paavo wasn't there.

15
The Kraken

Nobody was there. Not a soul, not a car moving in the street. Nothing.

So it was up to me to go down into the subway and unlock the door in the blue wall and let Jagiello out. And I couldn't do it.

I tried. I went partway down the steps.

I smelled the kraken stink, and I could hear the kraken moving deep in the tunnels. Its quarreling voices screamed and snarled among themselves as it heaved itself through the passages among the stopped trains. I stood there on the steps, hanging on to the wooden handrail with the key biting into my other palm, and I could not do it.

I started walking, not thinking where I was going, pushed along by a mean, blustery wind under that black sky. Next thing I knew I was outside my own apartment building, looking up at the window to my room. Miles and a short elevator ride away.

A woman in a bathrobe with her hair all wild was standing out in front staring down the street, her back to me. I walked softly, trying not to attract her attention—all I needed now was some street-crazy glomming on to me—but she must have heard something. She turned.

"Tina? Is that you?"

"Hi, Mom," I said.

"Where have you been?"

"Don't be mad, Mom," I said, backing up. "Everything's—" I was going to say, "okay," but that would have been such an outrageous lie that I couldn't get the word out.

"Everything's what?" she said. "And why should I be mad? Just because you've been missing for two days and a night? Not a word to me or anyone, just gone? Driving me entirely frantic and sending me blubbering to the police like a crazy woman? Mrs. Dermott called me. Who is this man you went to see Granny Gran with? My God, it was bad enough when I thought you'd run away with that Wechsler boy! I phoned his parents when I realized you were gone, and they really loved telling me that their precious Joel was gone too, believe me. They've never heard of this so-called musician, this old bum that the two of you have been hanging out with, getting into God knows what kind of trouble. So help me, I don't know what I've done to deserve this!

"Now you show up looking like a refugee in the middle of the night—"

"Mom, it's only dinnertime."

"No, it isn't," she said. "It's zero hour."

She started toward me. If I let her get hold of me, that would be that. It wouldn't be my fault that I couldn't go down into the subway with the key. It would be my mom's decision; I was only a kid, after all, and she was my mother.

But I backed away from her. My feet seemed to move on their own.

She stopped. She stood up tall, which isn't easy when you're only an inch over five feet and getting a little round besides, and she said with this shaky calm that made me really nervous, "Well, are you coming upstairs with me? Or did you only come back here to see how crazy you've driven me?" She'd been crying a lot. Her eyes were all swollen and red, without any mascara or anything for once. I felt bad for her.

"Listen, Mom," I said, "I'll come upstairs, in a minute. But there's something I have to do first."

That was the first I knew that I was going back down into that station, which was maybe why I was whimpering with fear while I said this.

"No, there isn't," she said in the same grim voice, only a little higher now. "All you have to do, young lady, is march yourself over here to me and into the elevator and into your room, where you will explain yourself to me with such conviction and burning truth that I may, I just may, at some point far in the future of your career as my child—for whom I am responsible—" (she screamed that part) "someday I may let you out again by yourself."

I backed up some more, feeling the key digging into my palm. I felt so sad for her—and for me—because there was nothing she could do and she didn't even know it. I was the one who knew how things stood, and there was nobody who could do anything except me at this point. I said, "I'm sorry, Mom, I can't."

"What do you mean, you can't?" she said. "You come here to me this minute!"

I shook my head, my sight all blurry with tears. "I can't, Mom. Going home won't help, it isn't safe. No place is safe. If I don't finish what I have to do, terrible things are going to happen to the whole world."

Mom stood there with her hands in fists and she opened her mouth and shrieked at me, "What the hell are you talking about? You are a fourteen-year-old schoolgirl! You get over here *this minute!*"

She lunged at me.

I ran. I could hear her coming after me in her slippers, swearing, and crying. She yelled my name, she yelled "Fire" and "Police," anything that might bring somebody out to help her stop me. She's no dope, my mom.

I cut down an alleyway and through a passage to the courtyards in the middle of the block, which I ran like a maze. Somehow I shinnied up the iron gate to the alley on the next street over and I raced for the Eighty-first Street station. Mom would have to go around half the block to intercept me, even if she knew where I was headed. She didn't stand a chance.

I dove down the steps of the Eighty-first Street station. The lady in the token booth yelled as I ducked under the turnstile. I skinned down the final steps onto the lower platform and into the hot, billowing stink of the kraken.

The whole uptown station was boiling black, the lights glimmering dimly through. It was only a few yards to the blue door on my left. I hesitated, trying to see, trying not to breathe, praying that somehow the kraken—it must be there, in the heart of that gritty, coiling heat—would not notice me, praying that I would find Paavo waiting here for me, ready to take over.

I could just see, through the dirty air, the door to Jagiello's prison. As I started toward it, out of the corner where the smoke had hidden them strolled the three Princes of Darkness.

My own momentum carried me right into Tattoo's chest. He grabbed me and laughed in my face—I smelled breath spray, can you believe that?—and the other two closed in.

I could either freeze like a rabbit and lose everything, or I could move.

I jerked my knee up as hard as I could, the way they tell you to in self-defense manuals. Tattoo went "Whuff!" and jackknifed so hard his chin collided painfully with my collarbone. He dropped. The other two were right behind him, laughing and jeering at him and at me, and there was no way I could get past them. None.

I saw shimmering movement at the blue door. I saw a figure take form in front of it, someone shadowy and barely visible like a person standing behind a sheet of water—or a waterfall in a vestpocket park in midtown.

Paavo—in some form, by some magic, it was Paavo. He reached upward with both hands, palms turned toward me, inviting.

I jumped back and swung my arm and I threw the key with all my strength.

As it spun through the air the Chewer made a grab for it. He missed. I saw the water shadow's hand snatch the

key from the air, and then the blue door opened a crack
and the wavering figure vanished inside. The door shut
again in the blink of an eye, as if it had never opened.

I was left there alone in the station with the Princes
and the screeching, snarling voices of the kraken.

"Okay," Pins-and-Grins said softly. "Now we're going to take care of you."

The Chewer took the gum out of his mouth and stuck
it on the wall and moved toward me. Tattoo was kneeling
on the platform, groaning, with his hands jammed between his legs. We all ignored him.

There was no place left for me to back to.

I was outraged. I could not believe it: I'd done it, I'd
delivered the key, I'd done my part in saving the world,
and I was about to be massacred anyway. The Chewer
held a knife in his hand, the bright, sharp edge turned
upward, toward me. Magic or no magic, I was going to get
sliced up by a thug, me, Valentine Marsh. Unbelievable. I
couldn't breathe at all because if I did, I would start to
scream.

From behind the blue steel wall came a clanging like
hammers on anvils. As we all stared, the whole front of the
wall groaned and screeched and tore away from its
moorings. It fell slowly, with a long, thundering crash, on
the platform.

Out of the dark behind it a horse and rider charged.
It was Jagiello.

Pins grabbed for me—to use me as a shield, I think—
but I twisted away and jumped behind a stanchion. He
dodged the big bronze shoulder of the horse, but the horse cur-

vetted sideways right into him. Too quickly for him to yell, Pins fell off the edge of the platform into the smoke.

Tattoo, crouching near the horse's feet, had yanked a length of chain from inside his jacket. He lashed out with it—I heard the chain rattle against the horse's foreleg—and then the horse reared back and stomped down with both front hooves. Tattoo fell with a squawk like a squashed parrot and lay there curled over with his mouth wide open, trying to get some air.

The Chewer grabbed hold of the drapery hanging over the horse's rump and scrambled up behind Jagiello. He flung one arm around the king's neck and jabbed wildly at the bronze face with his knife. The blade made a horrible screeching sound of metal on metal.

Jagiello bent forward and heaved upward out of the saddle, and the Chewer was smacked hard against the ceiling of the station. His knife clattered down and bounced off Jagiello's knee. The king shook himself hard and the Chewer slid off him like a sack of mud. Jagiello's horse stamped and skittered, throwing its head and snorting like a kettledrum.

There was a sound like something bigger than the world hissing its breath in. I saw Tattoo, still squirming, dragged toward the edge of the platform by a hazy loop of black, pulsing air. The limp body of the Chewer slid across the platform too, toward the tracks.

The kraken was retreating, pulling the Princes with it. Tattoo stared at me as he was dragged past. His lips made the word *help,* and blood leaked out of his mouth.

I reached toward him, I think.

Jagiello's crossed swords came down between Tattoo and me.

One after the other, the two remaining Princes dropped off the platform, and there was this sudden silence. I thought I'd gone deaf. The light glinted on Jagiello's swords, still lowered in front of me. The darkness was gone from the air.

"Climb up," the statue said, or anyway I heard the words "climb up."

I was scared to look at him. Even looming low over me like that, bent from the saddle, he was too big for the station.

Climb up? Where in Shakespeare does anybody say that?

But when a king tells you to do something, you know what? You do it. I put my foot on the crossing of the broad blades, grabbed his striped metal sleeve, and pulled myself up onto his horse's rump. With both arms stretched as far as they would go, I could hang on by hugging Jagiello and a lot of crumpled bronze drapery, his cloak. The metal of him was warm.

The horse's hooves rang like bells as it turned and galloped up the steps with me and the king stretched low on its neck to avoid the ceiling. We veered toward the turnstile, the bronze feet slipping a little on the concrete of the upper platform. I wanted to shut my eyes, but I couldn't: we had no clearance for a jump.

We crashed straight through the exit gates and lunged up the steep stairs to the street. I heard this wild scream from the token booth behind us.

Outside, it was full, black night. We took off across the avenue. I heard brakes and a man's shout, and the horse leaped over a white van and then over the low stone wall bordering the park.

I couldn't breathe, the wind whipped my hair into my eyes, and I was going to be too sore to walk tomorrow if there was a tomorrow. I didn't care.

Jagiello aimed the crossed swords above the horse's outstretched neck as if he steered with them instead of the reins. We raced downhill, across the bridle path, and up the long slope past the Shakespeare Gardens. Sparks flew up around the driving legs of the horse. We galloped in our own thunder, and overhead the clouds swung away from the face of a bright, full moon.

I hung on for dear life, yelling the way you do on a roller coaster, to let the terror and the joy out of you and to feel brave. Up the hill to the top, and there was the big playing field opening up on our left, the Delacorte Theatre wall like a huge wooden barrel curving on our right, and the lake—

The lake, silver gray in the moonlight, was boiling and seething.

The king pulled the horse up.

"Get down," he said. He stuck one leg out. I held onto his bronze belt with both hands, put my foot on his instep, and swung down.

My legs wouldn't hold me. I landed on my butt on the pavement, feeling like a fool.

But nothing could spoil that moment, nothing.

The bronze horse shook its mane and flared its nostrils and sprang away down the strip of grass alongside the lake, heading for Jagiello's empty plinth all the way at the other end. The horse would leap up into its place, the raised swords would do their magic and quiet the frothing water of the lake, and the kraken would be banished from my world. We had won.

Something reared up out of the water, up and up and up.

It was huge and glistery wet in the moonlight, black as ink, and roaring. Water streamed off it, and its eyes were hot red sparks set high in its towering shape. Everything shimmered behind the steam that flowed off the creature's black-bright hide. The kraken had come.

I covered my ears, not to hear the chittering-snarling, which was now a roaring, but I couldn't stop looking, I couldn't close my eyes.

The thick neck of Jagiello's horse doubled and its feet skidded on the turf. The centaur-king turned to face the kraken with his crossed blades raised. He shouted in a voice like the bells of a hundred steeples. If there were words, I didn't hear them.

Then he lowered the swords and uncrossed them so that the points were aimed straight over the horse's bent neck and at the kraken. He charged into the lake.

Sheets of water shot up from the plunging bronze hooves—and the horse stopped, swayed, almost fell. It dragged one hoof free with a fat, sucking sound, and I realized that its great heavy feet must be caught in the mucky lake bottom.

I saw the kraken arch over them both. The horse threw its metal head and strained its huge shoulders. Jagiello stood high in his stirrups, his body curved taut like the horse's body, because of course they were one being, one great, mired, doomed figure.

I found something heavy in my pocket. It was Granny Gran's chain-link purse full of silver dollars. It hefted beautifully. I hauled back and fired it off as hard as I could, and it smacked that coiling mass somewhere high up and stuck there.

The kraken voices shrieked, the sparky little eyes turned and glittered in my direction.

It breathed at me.

Not fire, just an incredible hot stench rolling over me that could have suffocated a dinosaur. I wanted to throw up and my eyes streamed tears.

I grabbed what I thought was a rock lying at the base of a tree—I think it was a little kid's shoe, actually—and I threw that too. I yelled, "Kraken, kraken, dirty, lousy, rotten kraken, stinking kraken, come and get me!"

It came. I caught a glimpse of the bronze horse-and-rider struggling back toward shore, and then the kraken's bulk blotted out the sight. It blotted out the little castle, and the southern skyline of tall light-spangled buildings outside the park, and the skyful of shifting clouds and washed-out stars, and everything.

The kraken heaved itself partway out of the lake and up onto the grass. The worse part was the awful noise it made, this hoarse, hungry, hateful breathing. It hissed in its breath, and if I hadn't had a lamppost to hang onto, I'd have been sucked right up into its dirty black mouth.

It clashed its jaws together.

I kicked over the trash basket chained to the lamppost, grabbed up some empty soda bottles and threw them.

One, two, three bottles.

The kraken heaved another coil of itself over the grass toward me. Two bottles left, nothing else—everything comes in those weightless cans now. When it opened its mouth to inhale again, I was done for anyhow.

Where was Jagiello? Where was Paavo? Where was anybody?

I was really going to die.

I could see better now. The kraken was coated with mud and slime and chunks of trash, with huge flat plates of broken concrete from under the lake bottom stuck all over it like scales. I could make out the wreck of a baby carriage riding high on one side of its head (if that was a head) like an ear. I could see splinters of glass gleaming and bicycle bars like horns. Its open mouth split down and down and down its reared-up bulk. It was all mouth except for the sparky little eyes that were bike reflectors, I think, red plastic embedded in mud.

It had teeth. I saw the moonlight gleam on them. Spokes of bicycle wheels, pieces of wire and jaggedy rods from crates, junk that people had thrown into the lake over the years, were stuck into the edges of the mouth like the baleen of a whale, gappy and rusty and raw-looking.

Tetanus, I thought, heaving another bottle. One touch and I've got tetanus, I'm dead anyhow.

My throwing arm was gone. I couldn't lift it at all.

I tried to run. My shoes slipped on the grass where the kraken had dripped slime and down I went.

On one knee I watched the thing haul back to swoop down and grab me. I tried to drown its crowing, whooping voice with a scream of my own, a scream wild and strong enough to power a final throw, with my left arm.

The last bottle flew wide, of course. Beautifully wide. It hit something that rang out a glorious, clear note. It was Jagiello, his horse's legs trailing weeds and wet paper trash from the lake as he came pounding at last over the grassy bank.

No war cry this time, just a hurtling figure with his swords pointing straight forward. Moonlight glinted on his crown and bent back, and the heavy bronze folds of his cloak lifted out behind him. The horse leaped like a train jumping the track at full speed and slammed into the monster headlong, right between two of the great, clumsy concrete scales.

The kraken's mouth gaped like a split in the sky as the monster stretched swaying and squalling above me. Then, moonlight shining on its ragged, rusty teeth, the kraken dove down, but not at me.

With a tearing, crunching sound, it plucked Jagiello out of its side. Still screaming, it lifted the centaur-king high against the moon, horse and rider caught in jaws like railway cars. The horse's legs kicked and threshed and

Jagiello's upper body arched back out of the grinding mouth.

Then the kraken toppled and its screaming ended in a ground-shaking crash.

Silence, a ringing, vibrating silence. Someplace beyond the park, I heard a bus grind its gears. The clouds had scattered, and the moon was very bright. Now I could see the towers of the city glittering with lights around the borders of the park. I could see the little castle sitting neatly on its crag, and the wall of the empty theater at one end of the lake, and Jagiello's empty plinth at the other.

At my feet, something vast and rotten-smelling shrank and drained away. All that bulk melted in front of my eyes, with no more sound than the trickling of water running back into the lake. Nothing was left but a huge dark stain on the grass. Bits of junk stuck up here and there, as if left on a beach by a slimy ebb tide.

One of the bits of junk was a big, twisted hunk of metal with two horse-legs sticking out into the night sky.

I stumbled over to the remains of Jagiello.

The statue was mangled and crushed. What looked like splashes of blood were really rips in the bronze where it had been gashed open by the kraken's jaws, showing the darkness of the hollow inside. The head of the horse was an unrecognizable mash of metal.

Jagiello's torso lay propped on one shoulder on the grass, at an ugly angle to the bulk of the ruined horse. His arms were all crumpled together with the blades of his swords. Something hung off one of the points of his crown, covering his face: a soggy leather cap with enameled metal pins stuck all over it. I pushed the cap off with a stick.

The face wasn't marked, except for a scratch on one blank bronze eye, from the Chewer's knife. An odd-shaped eye, with an Oriental fold over the upper lid—

I wasn't looking at the crude, middle-aged face of the statue I knew so well, with that smug mouth and comic-book scowl. This was another face, lined and old and fixed in a pain-twisted glare of grim determination. It was Paavo's face.

Now I knew how he had gotten the statue of Jagiello moving.

I cried, though crying was too small, somehow. I sat there sort of holding the hurt side of his face, half to hide, half to try to comfort that blank, scratched eye. I shut my own eyes and willing myself to stop living.

Inside my head came faint music. I didn't exactly *hear* it. It was like music coming straight into my mind without passing through the air at all: pure sounds, sweet and warm and chiding me a little. They sang my name: "Val. Valentine."

Then the bronze under my hand went cold.

I snatched my hand away and opened my eyes.

I saw only Jagiello's heavy, foolish face, a statue's face, and not a very good statue at that.

16

Gifts

The front door to our apartment was open. Mom stood there leaning against the jamb.

I wobbled out of the elevator to her and I said, "Mom, I'm back."

She slapped me so hard that I saw stars. "You ran away from me!"

I just stood there rocking. She grabbed me and hugged me, crying into my hair that it was just anxiety that made her hit me, being out of her mind with worry.

When you've had a kraken kill somebody you loved and nearly kill you, a smack from your mother—even a real belt—comes across differently. I hugged her back because it seemed like the right thing to do, though to tell the truth I wasn't feeling much of anything. In a tired, far-off sort of way, I was sorry to have put her through so much.

Any other time I would have cried, too, but I was all wrung dry. I just waited until she was done. By then she'd gotten my hair and cheek wet enough for both of us anyhow.

"Are you all right?" she was babbling, pulling me with her into the dark hall of the apartment. "Did anybody hurt you? My God, baby, you're covered with mud, you look as if a bus ran over you! What happened? Why did you run away from me tonight? Where did you go? Tina, for heaven's sake, what's been *happening?*"

Being called "baby" didn't bother me a bit, I noticed in a detached way, while all sorts of possible lies flashed through my head: I ran away because I was doing badly in school and I couldn't stand how upset it made you. I ran away to live in the park and get material for a terrific paper for Mr. Chernick's creative writing class. Spies kidnaped me, mistaking me for a diplomat's daughter. I ran away to make you pay attention to me. Standard stuff.

But I did not want to lie to my mother. Something serious had happened. Now that she couldn't put a stop to it anymore I wanted her to know, because it had been important to me.

I said, "Mom, I've got something to tell you that you're going to think is crazy, but I think you should hear it. First, though, I'm okay. I'm only a little bruised and skinned and tired, I'm not hungry, and I must still be the only kid in my grade who doesn't do drugs."

"One thing, Tina," she said, still holding me by both shoulders as if she was afraid I'd run off again if she let go. "Is Joel's disappearance connected with all this at all? Because if it is, I'd better call his parents right away. They've been frantic. And I should call the police, too, and tell them you're back."

I said, "I think Joel is okay. And I think you should hear the whole thing before you talk to anybody."

"You know," she said, "I thought I was worried before, but this tone you're taking is scaring the hell out of me. Okay, tell me. I can take it. I'm listening."

She could take it all right, but she couldn't believe it, not right away.

I edited a little about Paavo and me because *a,* she'd have killed me; and *b,* I'd rather have died than told her my real feelings about him; and *c,* as it was, I could hardly say his name without choking up and going all achy inside with misery.

When I was finished I sat there on the living room couch wondering when I was going to fall over into a dead sleep, which would be a terrific relief. Mom sat with me, gnawing on her knuckles. Finally she said, "Let's go over to that subway stop."

"I don't think I can," I said. "I'm tired, Mom."

She stood up. "I'll go myself, then."

I said, "Don't go into the park, though, all right? The kraken's gone and the Princes too, but there are still plenty of crazies and meanies wandering around."

And I keeled right over.

I slept until the middle of the next day. Mom came into the living room when she heard me stirring. She didn't say anything. She handed me the newspaper and went back in the kitchen.

I was glad she had stayed home from work because I felt sort of all disconnected. I wouldn't have eaten or dressed or anything without somebody getting me moving in this direction or that one. I mean it was good, being taken care of.

And I knew as long as she was there I wasn't going to break down and think about Paavo, and that was fine. I didn't want to think about him. I didn't want to cry over him any more than I had right there on the grass the night before, because it hurt and it didn't do any good.

The papers were full of this crazy mystery of a "vandalized" subway station. The token booth person was in a hospital, under sedation, and described as "in shock." I bet. Then there was the discovery of the remains of Jagiello, looking as if he'd been crunched in an earthquake, and the messed up wiring in the subway system and the traffic lights, and a few other things. Mysteries.

All the things that were missing had returned to their places when Jagiello came busting out of the blue wall. Which left us with two medicine cabinets trying to share the same wall space in Mom's bathroom; and there were all those mail chutes and things. Mom and the landlord came to some sort of straggling truce. This pleased Mom. She at least has some idea of what went on, and he didn't have a clue and still doesn't. About the return of my bookbag with a many-days-old tuna fish sandwich in the bottom of it, the less said the better.

I don't know whether Paavo's cap turned up anyplace. Most likely some old derelict took it, as Paavo had thought, and he's welcome to it.

At lunch that day Mom sat across the table and stared at me over her cup of coffee, while I picked at some grapefruit she'd cut for me.

"Joel's mother called," she said. "She says he came in this morning and told them he got fed some kind of dope by practical jokers at school and went wandering off in a daze. He won't give any names and they're not going to pursue it. I don't know about his other talents, but he's certainly a champion liar."

I was sorry Joel didn't think he could tell his parents the truth, but if that was the only way he could handle it with them, I didn't want us to mess it up for him. I said, "You didn't say anything to his mother about what I told you?"

She grimaced. "I didn't say anything about that to anybody, and I'm not going to. I hope you won't either."

I shook my head and poked at the grapefruit.

"You know, Tina," she said, "your Granny Gran used to say that she'd seen the Loch Ness monster once, while she was out picking flowers or something. She didn't fuss about it or go around telling people in general, but she told me. Just once."

"Is that why you believe me?" I said.

"No. I believe you because I guess I'm in the habit of believing you," she said, and she leaned over and kissed my forehead, which made me feel shaky and embarrassed. "And because if it is the kind of thing that runs in families, better you than me, my dear. I'm not sure I could handle it as well as you're handling it."

She could handle it. She's not as soft as she thinks.

She took me to the doctor that afternoon to have me checked over, and I spent the next couple of days resting in bed.

Joel called from a phone booth someplace, but it didn't cost him much. It was a short call.

"Tina!" he said. "You're really all right?"

"Yes, I guess so," I said. "Joel, can you see?"

"Sure I can see. I saw that mess in the park, for one thing. Jesus! What happened? Where's Paavo?"

Tears started running out of my eyes. "He's dead," I said.

"What?"

"I said he's dead. The kraken killed him."

After a minute he said, "But we won. The kraken's gone. He can't be dead!"

"He's dead, Joel. He made himself into Jagiello, and the kraken came out of the lake. I threw some bottles at it, and he charged into it and it died. But he died too. It killed him as it died. I saw it happen." I felt as if I was killing Paavo all over again every time I said "died" or "dead," and I knew it hurt Joel to hear it but I didn't care.

"He's not dead!" he shouted. "You're lying!"

I couldn't talk anymore because I was crying too hard. I hung up. Joel didn't call back.

So a hard part of all this was not having anyone my age to talk with about it. I tried to tell Barbara once, but she had no time for fairy tales, she said. And I never considered telling Megan. She wouldn't understand about me and Joel, let alone me and Paavo. There's no way I can see myself trying to explain it to her. Not until she grows up a little, anyhow.

Even Mom wouldn't talk about it much with me afterward. Sometimes I got the feeling this was because she was just a little bit jealous.

Another thing, about friends.

Word got around school, of course, all completely cockeyed but fascinating to people. The story agreed on by my mom and Joel's parents was that I had run away because of my grades in math, and that Joel had come after me to try to keep me out of trouble. We said we'd hung around in the subways and the park until we got too hungry to stick it out any longer, and then we'd come home. People seemed to believe this, but some of them— the wrong ones, of course—wanted more.

Kim Larkin came around one day and said to me, "Where did you and this Joel hole up? What happened?" She and some of her pals sat down at my lunch table. I got the distinct impression that they were expecting me to try to buy my way into their group, at long last, with juicy secrets about me and "this Joel."

I also had the feeling that I would rather cut my throat than feed any of that part of my life into their greedy little shining faces.

I said, "My guidance counselor says it's better for me not to talk about it."

"Oh," said Kim, shaking her hair back like a model, "that bad, huh? Well if it's something you two can't talk about to anybody else, I guess you'll be talking just to each other from now on, right? If 'talking' is what you call it."

Amy, the freckled one, started making disgusting wet kissy noises. The rest giggled. Other kids were watching us and whispering.

"Where is this Joel?" Kim said, looking around with this slinky look. "Nobody I know has ever seen him. What happened, did he disappear into the quicksand of the swamp?"

Amy said, "I bet Lennie murdered him in a jealous fit."

"And threw his body in the *swamp,*" Kim crowed.

All of a sudden I got very tired of the whole thing. I sat back and looked her in the eye and I said, "Kim, you're pretty and you're smart and you're popular and your parents have enough money to dress you nicely and send you to Europe to ski at Christmas. How come with all those advantages you act like such a horse's ass?"

They all looked as shocked as if I'd kicked them.

Then Kim came back with, "Well, Swampy, you're dumb and you're ugly and you've got no friends and you dress like a reject from the Salvation Army, so how come with all your disadvantages you don't go drown yourself?"

The weirdest thing happened. A giggle bubbled out of me and I started to laugh a good, loud laugh. It felt great.

Then I just folded my arms and just looked at her, smiling and feeling good for the first time in days. Pretty soon she and her friends got bored sitting around going yuk yuk and trying to get anything more out of me, and they took off.

They haven't bothered me since. In fact, a couple of girls who are kind of fringe members of Kim's clique, sometimes in and sometimes out, have started trying to hang around with Barbara and me. Soon there'll be an invitation to a party or something, I can see it coming. Now that it doesn't matter a bit to me, the whole problem evaporates. Weird.

Mom and I went to see Granny Gran. I don't know what I expected, but anyway, she looked the same as always. She smiled at my mother and asked her to please go away and let us talk alone.

Mom said, "Whatever you two have to say to each other, in view of—what Valentine says happened, I think I have a right to hear."

Granny Gran said, "What about that shortcake I asked you for last time?"

Mom set her jaw and glared from one of us to the other and back again. I sat there being miserable and silent, and Granny Gran hummed to herself. Finally Mom got up and went away to talk to Mrs. Dermott.

Granny Gran looked hard at me. "Well?" she said.

"He died, Gran," I said.

"Who did?"

I started to cry because all of a sudden I was thinking about Paavo, which I hadn't been able to do much lately. Every time I'd tried, my mind went blasting off in some other direction as if I'd burned it on something. But now he was right there, and that burned, all right. Knowing he only existed in my thoughts and not in reality anymore really burned.

"Well, who, Val? Don't just sit there blubbering. A lot of people have died, you know. At my age it seems as if that's all anybody does, practically." Then she said, "Oh, you must mean Paavo Latvela," and she sighed and patted my hand with her knotty old fingers that could barely pick anything up anymore.

It all poured out of me in a flood, including the parts I'd censored from my mom.

Granny Gran sat patting my hand and listening and nodding, and after a while she put one bumpy-knuckled finger against my lips and told me, "Hush now, that's enough. He'd be embarrassed. You wouldn't want to embarrass him, would you? He was always a little shy, you know, a little nervous about strong feeling. That took a lot, him talking to you as straight as he did about attachments to people. And it was good sense, too, what he told you. I didn't know he knew that much about such things. About monsters and the like, yes, but people's hearts, well, that's a surprise."

Shy! Paavo, shy? It's very hard when someone else turns out to know something you don't, something personal and important, about somebody you thought you got to know pretty intimately. Especially when you'll never have a chance now to find out that kind of thing about him for yourself.

"How can you just sit and talk about him like that?" I said. "I'm telling you he's dead, Gran! I was with him and I didn't even know what was going on until it was all over. I didn't know Jagiello was him!"

"Well, of course it was him," she said a little testily. "You didn't think that a brainless, hollow-hearted, soulless bronze statue could take on a kraken, did you? Keep one out, yes, but fight one once the kraken was loose and moving? Never. Of course Paavo Latvela had to take over himself, and naturally he couldn't do it in that elderly human body he was wearing, pleasing though it was. It was pleasing, wasn't it? He was always fine-looking, in whatever form I knew him, but without ostentation. Great style, Paavo Latvela had. Thoughtful of him, too, not to let you know that he was moving Jagiello. After all, what could you have done besides what you did do, had you known?"

Well, off I went blubbering again, knowing she was right. There was nothing else I could have done, not a thing.

"Did you know?" I said, struck by a sudden horrible possibility. "Did you know he was going to do it that way and let him go off and do it?"

"Well, no, lovie," she said softly. "I don't think I could have managed that. I have some kinds of sight—I did see the ending, you know—but not that kind, not prediction, thank heaven."

"You saw what happened at the lake?" I said. "How?"

"Why, in my bathroom basin, which I had filled with water. He used water to call me, because he needed my help to distract the kraken when you were looking for Joel. He had his hands full himself with the Princes, who were following his water shadow all over town, wherever he led them. I used the basin to concentrate and send some of the stored-up charge from here. Most of it I got from the cribbage game on the porch there. I made the kraken think that an army from Sorcery Hall was arriving through the Lincoln Tunnel. Off the brute went to do battle, leaving you free to contact Joel. That was about the limit of what I could manage, but it served, didn't it?

"I stayed by the water and watched the rest: a great and terrible ending for Paavo Latvela. I did my crying then, you see. I couldn't put it off for fear I might not be spared the time to do it later."

That pulled me up short: the thought of maybe losing Granny Gran too. I thought I would suffocate on my bitter feelings.

"Anyway, lovie, he did what he set out to do, didn't he? I'm sorry it cost so much, but I know he'd rather have paid the price than failed."

True, I knew it was true. "Oh Gran," I said. "But he's gone, and I have nothing at all to remember him by. Sometimes I can hardly even think what he looked like, I mean clearly."

"Time will cure that," she said a little grimly. "When you're old like me, lovie, you'll remember every hair of his fine head and feed your tired heart on those memories. But for now, it's just as well, you see, because he's gone and shouldn't be haunting you, now should he? Getting in your way, taking your attention from what's going on around you? Why, you could be busy remembering Paavo Latvela and walk in front of a bus!"

"Gran!" I said. I was really shocked. "You don't mean I should deliberately forget him! He was wonderful, he treated me like a grown-up, he was—"

"Just don't fight against it, that's all," she said, "the blurring effect of time, I mean. You can't fight that any more than you can fight the growth of your bones, lovie."

"I can," I said. "I'll find some way to remember."

"And he did leave you something," she added.

I stared at her, wondering if he'd given her something for me, something she'd been keeping to give me now that it was all over. Past her shoulder I could see Mom coming back with Mrs. Dermott.

"What, Gran?" I said, "Quick, give it to me before Mom comes!"

"It's your name, lovie," she said softly. "What did Paavo Latvela call you?"

I said, "He called me Val, or Valentine."

"Not Tina, the little doll, the baby," Gran said. "Val. Val for Valor. Valentine for love."

And then Mom was saying, "Are you two ready to let anybody else into this conversation?" She was looking sharply at me, noticing that I'd been crying, of course.

Granny Gran said, "We were about to invite you, but I can't find the phone number, dear." Mom gave up. But I had my gift.

So back to Joel, I guess. This is hard because it should have turned out differently, or that's how I felt. We'd been through enormous danger together, and I expected something strong and permanent between us, a bond, because of it.

Well, maybe that's what I got, but not in the form I expected.

A day came when I figured I'd better go make my peace with the fact that Paavo Latvela was dead but that ugly, dumb statue was back in its place again. They'd made a copy of Jagiello and set him up on his pedestal again, on the terrace at the east end of the lake. I knew because I'd read about it in the papers. I hadn't walked across the park after school since that night. I'd been taking the bus.

So one afternoon, on a warm day in late spring with the end of school in sight, I walked out on the black spur of rock in front of the terrace. For a while I watched some boys rapelling with khaki climbing ropes all over the cliff under the little castle at the other end of the lake. I felt nothing at my back where the new statue stood, no presence. I might have been standing anywhere.

Finally I turned around and walked between the two little old-fashioned lampposts (where Paavo had held himself up after the Princes jumped us that afternoon) and up the steps onto Jagiello's terrace under the trees. I looked up.

There he was, as ugly as ever: the lumpy horse in lumpy horse-drapery, with a twig caught on the little chain that links the bit to the single rein. The king was standing in his stirrups brandishing his crossed swords at the sky over the lake, with the hilt of a third sword showing at his left hip. Funny, I'd never noticed that third sword before. Imagine carrying three!

What bothered me was that there was no sign of what I knew had happened, nothing at all.

While I was standing there getting teary and mad, two guys came up and one of them asked me in a heavy French accent what the statute was.

"It's a monument to Jagiello, a medieval Polish king," I said.

They discussed this in French. Then the short one asked me, "What 'e doing zere?"

"Guarding the lake," I said. "Protecting us from monsters."

I walked away.

Somebody caught up with me, bu it wasn't one of the French guys. It was Joel.

He and I had not spoken together since that last phone call. We'd been avoiding each other.

He said, "Hi. I came to say good-bye."

"What?" I said. Why say good-bye to someone you never talked to anyway?

"I'm going up to Boston to stay with my aunt and uncle. I leave next week so I can settle in over the summer before term starts in my new school."

He looked very good, very slim and dramatically handsome. He was wearing jeans and a rugby shirt and a plaid scarf.

"It's too warm for a scarf," I said.

He got red in the face. He took off the scarf. There was the fiddler's brand on the side of his neck, fresh and sore-looking.

"I'm glad you're still playing," I said.

"I play like a pig," he said bitterly. "I don't even have his bow to use, did you know that? It burned up. I mean all of a sudden it flared, like a torch, and I could see again by the light it gave. That's how I found my way out of the damned subway where you left me. Though I nearly got run over by a northbound express."

"Joel," I said, "what's eating you? We won, you know? It cost us, but we won."

"*You* won," he said. "Wasn't it right around here that you killed the kraken with Coke bottles?"

"Oh boy, Joel," I said. This was really very painful, and I wished I'd taken the bus across town after all. "It was Paavo Latvela who killed the kraken and paid the price for it too. I was along for the ride, that's all."

"That's all," he mimicked. "Don't be so modest. It isn't every day that the damsel in distress goes to fight the dragon while the gallant knight sits waiting to be rescued from a crummy hologram of a subway station. While you were pulverizing the kraken, I strolled out of the subway with the ashes of that bow on my hand and a fiddle under my arm; not a mark on me. I might as well have been asleep the whole time."

I said, "Joel, if you'd gone and fought the kraken and come back the winner, I wouldn't be sulking and whining about it. I'd tell people you were a hero and we'd have a party."

"That's right," he said. "That's what you're supposed to do. You're a girl."

"Oh," I said.

"Oh. That's right. Think about it a minute."

"I am thinking. You're jealous."

"I'm not!" he said.

"Admit it, Joel. You're jealous!"

He wouldn't look at me. Suddenly he hauled off and smacked his fist into the tree next to us. Then he stood there hugging his hand and yelling, "You had no right! You're the girl, you're the one who should have been stuck in the subway! Who ever heard of a girl fighting a monster! It isn't fair!"

I shouted back. "What is this? I'm supposed to leave all the serious, exciting stuff for you to do because you're a boy? Hey, did you ever hear of such a thing as a human being? A human being, you know, a person? I'm one of those, though I happen to be a female-type human being. That means I do things for myself like anybody else, even if they happen to be dangerous things. Which I'd better be able to do, too, because there isn't always going to be some guy around to take care of it for me—like that night, for instance."

Which was a low blow, but he'd asked for it. Besides, it was his own fault he'd been stuck in the subway. Nobody had asked him to try to use the key instead of giving it to Paavo the way he was supposed to.

"You could have been killed!" Joel said murderously.

"But not you, right? Because you're stronger and smarter and better, right? Because a girl can't fight a kraken, or how will the boys be able to talk about how superior they are? I'm glad you play the violin like a pig, because you are a pig, Joel Wechsler—a selfish, greedy, macho pig!"

"And you're a nut," he snarled. He shook his hurt hand at me. "Look what you made me do! I can't play the violin with a broken hand!"

"Joel, nobody made you sock that tree. Nobody *made* you do anything, so don't give me that crap, all right?"

"It doesn't matter," he said, hugging his hand again and turning away from me. "I'm giving up the violin, I'm not going to play anymore."

"Oh, make up your mind," I said.

"I have. I'll quit. There's no point to it." Suddenly he swung around and yelled in my face, "He was going to teach me, I know I could have gotten him to teach me! I'll never find a teacher like him again, never in my whole life. He was an old man, and he didn't know his way around like regular New Yorkers, and he went up against a monster. And I wasn't there. And he died."

So that was it. If Joel had been there he could have changed things. Ha. I'd seen the kraken, and I knew differently. That alone made me not so mad at what he said but sorry for him, a little. Besides, I saw that his eyes were glittering with tears.

"Well, I was there," I said, "and I couldn't make it come out any differently. And I'm sorry."

I walked away. Joel didn't follow me. I felt, besides miserable sadness and anger, this pulling in my chest, under my heart. There should have been something between us, something besides jealousy and anger and mean words. There was, too. I felt it and I knew he felt it. Paavo didn't tell me what you do when you feel that pull and it's to somebody who causes you a lot of grief, even if it's mostly because that person is feeling a lot of grief himself.

Anyway, that was all I heard from Joel before he left.

Meantime, I've started seeing Lennie again, just a friendly sort of hanging around together. And there's a very nice guy, Brian, a new kid who only moved here last summer from North Carolina. I'm teaching him about New York, which he loves.

Yesterday, we walked across the park and sat down by the lake. A lady came by in front of us towing a little kid. She settled herself on the grass across the path from us and started to read, and the kid discovered a scoop of melting ice cream somebody had dropped on the pavement. He got down on all fours and started licking. We both stared, fascinated, sort of nudging each other with our elbows and wondering when the lady would wake up. She had her nose in one of those interchangeable romance novels that Megan is always trying to get me to read, so maybe the answer was, never, not on her own.

"The kid gets to finish the ice cream," Brian whispered to me.

I thought of all the times I got stopped from doing things I wanted to do for no good reason except the sixth sense my mother had had about stuff like that. "Nope," I said.

"How much?" Brian loves a bet.

"A nickel."

"A dime."

"Okay."

A man with a dachshund on a leash came by and stopped. He tipped his hat to the lady on the grass and pointed out to her that her kid was eating ice cream off the sidewalk. The lady smacked the kid, the kid began to scream, and the dachshund gobbled up the ice cream. Brian paid me a dime.

"Real New York," I said.

My New York, which the kraken didn't get to scarf up like that dog ate up the ice cream, because we didn't let it.

The other day I got a letter from Joel.

My hand wasn't broken, which is a good thing, since this school is for teaching music first, everything else second. They are tough up here. I've got calluses on my calluses and permanent cramps in my shoulders. If you don't practice all the time, you're dead. My teacher is great, but he keeps telling me there are no shortcuts: no magic formulas, he says. (You know who I wish he could talk to. Wish I could talk to that person too.) And then he piles on the assignments, because he says he thinks I'm "promising." What I'm promising is to kick myself around the block for letting myself in for all this. How's your writing?

Joel, trying to be less of a pig

P.S. Maybe you would consider coming to my rescue sometime?

Boston isn't so far. Maybe I will.

ABOUT THE AUTHOR

SUZY MCKEE CHARNAS is well known to readers of science fiction and fantasy. She is the author of *Walk to the End of the World* and *Motherlines*. Her novella *The Unicorn Tapestry* won a Nebula Award in 1980 and became the core of her third novel, *The Vampire Tapestry,* published the following year. She says that *The Bronze King* began with a vision of a wizards' clubhouse, something like the Harvard Club or the Yale Club in New York City, called Sorcery Hall. As her story developed, Sorcery Hall itself disappeared, but one of the sorcerers remained—a wizard of water magic and music magic, Paavo Latvela, whose powers were to triumph over the fearsome kraken.

Ms. Charnas lives in Albuquerque, New Mexico, and spends as much of her summer as she possibly can at the Santa Fe Chamber Music Festival.

Life is Not Always What You Expect After High School.

From Norma Johnston, Mystery and Romance You Won't Want to Put Down!

☐ **WHISPER OF THE CAT** 26947-X $2.95
(Coming in March)
On a misty lowlands island off the coast of Georgia, in a beautiful, sprawling mansion surrounded by dangerous swamp, 16-year-old Lacey Fairbrother finds a handsome, troubled young man, a sweet, mystic old lady, her silver Persian cat . . . and murder.

☐ **SHADOW OF A UNICORN** 26475-3 $2.95
When her mother's sudden death leaves 16-year-old Sarah Drake orphaned, she welcomes the invitation to go live with her cousin Rowena in Kentucky's bluegrass country. That is until Sarah learns of the curse on Unicorn Farms—a deadly legend dating back to the days of the French and Indian wars!

☐ **THE WATCHER IN THE MIST** 26032-4 $2.95
Cindy Clayborne is thrilled when she lands a summer job with her cousins at Rockcove Hall, the wonderful old inn right on the New England coast. But soon after her arrival horrifying things begin to happen, and people begin whispering about the Watcher, a lonesome spirit who walks the rocky shores.

DON'T MISS THESE OTHER SCARY BANTAM THRILLERS!

Special Offer
Buy a Bantam Book
for only 50¢.

Now you can order the exciting books you've been wanting to read straight from Bantam's latest catalog of hundreds of titles. *And* this special offer gives you the opportunity to purchase a Bantam book for only 50¢. Here's how:

By ordering any five books at the regular price per order, you can also choose any other single book listed (up to a $5.95 value) for only 50¢. Some restrictions do apply, so for further details send for Bantam's catalog of titles today.

Just send us your name and address and we'll send you Bantam Book's SHOP AT HOME CATALOG!